Praise for the Novels of H.J. Ralles

The Keeper Series

"Aimed at young adults, this is ingenious enough to appeal powerfully to adults who wonder how far this entire computer age can go. Ralles knows how to pace her story - the action moves in sharp chase-and-destroy scenes as Commanders hunt down the dangerous young boy. The characters are memorable, particularly the very human 101. And that ending . . . -is brilliant. A compelling read from exciting beginning to just as exciting ending." –**The Book Reader**

"*Keeper of the Kingdom* is a must read for children interested in computers and computer games. From the first page to the last there is no relief from the suspense and tension. H.J. Ralles has captivated anyone with a fascination for computer games, and has found a way to connect computer-literate children to reading." *–JoAn Martin, Review of Texas Books*

"Kids will be drawn into this timely sci-fi adventure about a boy who mysteriously becomes a character in his own computer game. The intriguing plot and growing suspense will hold their attention all the way through to the book's provocative ending." –**Carol Dengle, *Dallas Public Library***

"This zoom-paced sci-fi adventure, set in the kingdom of Zaul, is a literary version of every kid's dream of a computer game. Keeper of the Kingdom may be touted for youngsters from 9 to 13, but I'll bet you my Spiderman ring that it will be a "sleeper" for adults as well." –**Johanna M. Brewer, *Plano Star Courier***

"As in any good video game the PG-rated action is unrelenting, and the good guys never give up. *Keeper of the Kingdom* could be made easily into an adequate Nickelodeon-style kids' movie." *–VOYA*

"H.J. Ralles continues to offer readers a fascinating affiliation between computers and books. Her two 'Keeper' stories are wonderful reading experiences." *–The Baytown Sun*

"H.J. Ralles spins a wonderful Science Fiction tales aimed at younger readers, but has also created something that is quite enjoyable for book lovers of all ages." –**Conan Tigard, *ReadingReview.com***

"Ralles knows how to turn out a first-rate story. And, how to make coming-of-age as suspenseful as nature makes it every day." –**Lisa DuMond, *SFSite***

"*Keeper of the Empire* is a fun read, with action that grips you from the start. Excellent for middle school and reluctant readers; enjoyable and suspenseful." –**Christie Gibrich, Roanoake Public Library, Roanoke, Texas**

Darok Series

"*Darok 9* is an exciting post-apocalyptic story about the Earth's last survivors, barely enduring on the harsh surface of the moon . . . An enjoyable and recommended novel for science fiction enthusiasts."*–The Midwest Book Review*

"*Darok 9* has the excitement of a computer game, put into a book, that parents and teachers will love to see in the hands of their children." –**Linda Wills,** *Rockwall County News*

"*Darok 9* is another wonderful science fiction book for young adults by H.J. Ralles, author of Keeper of the Kingdom. Filled with nonstop action and suspense, it tells the story of a young scientist, Hank Havard, and his quest to keep his big discovery out of enemy hands. The language in this book is clean, as it was in Keeper of the Kingdom, something I found refreshing. Also, the message that violence doesn't pay is strong. The characters are believable, and the plot is solid. Darok 9 is a can't-put-it-down, go-away-and-let-me-read science fiction thriller, sure to please any reader of any age!" –**Jo Rogers,** *Myshelf.com*

"From the explosive opening chapter, the pace of Darok 9 never falters . . . Ralles holds us to the end in her tension-filled suspense. We read on to see what surprising events her interesting characters initiate. The scientific jargon and technology does not interfere with the action-filled story which any person can follow even if less versed in the science fiction aspects." –**JoAn Martin,** *Review of Texas Books*

"H.J. Ralles is the author and creator of this science fiction book for kids. However, Darok 9 certainly can hold its own in the adult world as well. This very entertaining book is hard to put down. Once you start reading it you just want to know how it will end. Filled with action and surprises around every bend this book keeps your attention." –**Kelly Hoffman,** *Slacker's Sci-Fi Source*

"In the near future, Earth has been ravaged by ecological and military disaster. The few who survived have gone to our Moon, eking out an existince in domed towns called Daroks (Domed AtmospheRic Orbital Kommunities). Our plucky protagonist is a scientist researching ways to reduce the need for water by humans. Little does he know that treachery and betrayal lay all about him. An attack on the remote lab by the Fourth Quadrant sets him running from more than just falling masonry . . the double-crosses and double-double-crosses should be engaging for a young adult. *–Space Frontier Foundation, Moon Book of the Month Club*

Keeper

of the

Colony

Keeper of the Colony

By

H.J. Ralles

Top Publications, Ltd.
Dallas, Texas

Keeper of the Colony

A Top Publications Paperback

First Edition
12221 Merit Drive, Suite 950
Dallas, Texas 75251

ISBN#: 1-929976-35-6
Library of Congress Control Number 2005910186

The characters and events in this novel are fictional and created out of the imagination of the author. Certain real locations and institutions are mentioned, but the characters and events depicted are entirely fictional.

Printed in the United States of America

For
Claire, Louise, Joanna and Philip

May you find the courage and vitality to pursue
your dreams.

Acknowledgements

Many thanks to: Malcolm, who never fails to rescue me from all my computer nightmares; Richard and Edward— my most patient and loyal supporters; Brenda Quinn, for the many hours of editing and attention to detail which made this book what it is; Bill Manchee and all at Top Publications, who continue to believe in The Keeper Series; my friends in the Plano Writers, the SCBWI and the NAWW whose critiquing skills are invaluable; and Motophoto, Plano, for great publicity photographs.

Chapter 1

Keir crept to the end of Fisherman's Alley, careful to stay hidden in the shadows of the crumbling buildings. He had less than five minutes to get home. He froze at the sound of the nine o'clock curfew bell. Fear rose in his chest. He still had two blocks to go. Now he was really in trouble!

He glanced nervously down Wharf Street and then back at the docks, trying to make out shapes in the mist. Thankfully there was no sound of the curfew patrol. He listened carefully, but all he heard was the gentle lapping of the seawater against the boat ramps and the occasional blast of a foghorn offshore. All seemed quiet in the Dark End of Javeer, but on a cold damp night like tonight he couldn't be certain.

Be careful, Keir, he reminded himself. *You're a runner for the Underground and many people are depending on you. Don't take a risk when you're nearly home.*

He took another look around the corner. *A sprint up the street should do it.* He pulled his knit hat lower over his wild black hair and turned his jacket collar up against the icy wind. Heart pounding furiously, he bravely stepped into the open.

What just moved across the street? Keir threw himself

back against the wall in panic. Instantly the skies above rumbled. Gunships! Their detectors had obviously picked up movement and now the curfew patrol was on its way. Had they seen him? He fought to keep calm.

The sky was suddenly ablaze with flashing red lights, and a deafening roar signaled the approaching gunships. Moments later the lumbering craft landed in the street. Blaring sirens sent shivers down Keir's spine. He stood against the wall and clenched his fists in preparation for combat. *Who am I kidding?* he thought. *I can't fight Gulden Guards armed with ST29s!* He held his breath as he waited for the Gulden Guards to show up and cuff him . . . but no one came.

He heard a scuffle in the street close by and dared to look around the corner. Several Gulden Guards surrounded an old man in a dark shirt and baggy pants, who was struggling to free himself from chains around his ankles and wrists. "Who are you people? Where are you taking me? Why don't you answer?" he snarled, snatching at the cuffs.

Doesn't he know about the Gulden Guards? thought Keir. He didn't recognize the man, although it was hard to make out faces on a night like tonight. Perhaps this was a stranger who didn't know any better, but he couldn't imagine anyone choosing to come here. No one in his right mind would visit the Colony of Javeer. He watched as the Gulden Guards shoved the old man into one of the metallic green gunships. With engines thundering, it took off as quickly as it had landed.

Keir's legs were still shaking as the engine noise subsided. He sat against the wall until his heart resumed its normal rhythm, and once again he considered the short run home. With any luck the curfew patrol wouldn't return to his neighborhood for at least fifteen minutes.

He drew in a deep breath and tore across the street to the abandoned buildings on the other side. The most dangerous part of his journey was over. The rest should be easy—as long as he stayed in the shadows.

Suddenly something bumped him from behind. "Hey!" Keir shouted, turning to see a boy in the middle of the sidewalk. "Watch where you're going!"

The boy shrank back. Keir instantly realized he'd been too loud, and shoved the boy sideways into the doorway of the old First Bank of Boro.

"Hey! Get your hands off me!" said the boy angrily.

"Shh!" said Keir, his heart racing again. He slapped his hand over the boy's mouth and checked around for the curfew patrol. He listened for a few seconds. Except for the distant foghorn, the night was still quiet. No rumbling skies or flashing lights this time.

Keir sighed heavily and pulled his hand away. "What do you think you're doing?" he whispered angrily. "Do you want the Gulden Guards to catch us?"

"Who? What are you talking about?" replied the boy, his teeth chattering.

Keir studied him, hardly knowing what to think. The boy wore only a thin jacket and shoes that weren't fit for winter weather. He was just a little taller than Keir himself, and was probably about the same age. "You must have heard the bell," said Keir. "There's a nine o'clock curfew in the Dark End and we've already broken it. Go home. Now!"

The boy seemed confused. "The Dark End? Curfew? But I don't have anywhere to go . . . I just got here . . . and I'm already half frozen." He shuffled from foot to foot and rubbed his hands together.

Keir stared at him for a few seconds. This didn't make any sense. This was the second stranger he'd seen in just a few minutes. One thing was certain, it was too risky to stand here and interrogate this boy further, but his gut instinct told him that the boy was lost and needed protecting. Keir wouldn't leave anyone to the fate of the Gulden Guards. He'd have to trust him. "You'd better come home with me," he said, grabbing his arm.

"Thanks for the offer," the boy muttered, shaking him free, "but I've got to find my friends . . . and fast! Don't suppose you've seen an old man and a thin boy about our age, have you?"

Keir gritted his teeth in frustration. After all his worries about taking home a stranger, now the boy was refusing to come! "Look, you obviously don't get it," he said in a forced whisper. "We'll be arrested if we don't get off the streets *right now*!"

The boy finally seemed to hear. "Really?"

"*Really*," Keir stressed. "I mean it! We have to get out of here."

The stranger looked flustered. "Okay . . . right . . . I'll

come then. Is it far?"

"Less than two blocks. Stay behind me, don't make any noise and keep in the shadows. You got it?"

"Sure. Anything you say."

After a quick look into the street, Keir set out briskly toward his home. He led the boy into the alleyway between the old candy factory and the abandoned warehouse that was now his home . . . if it could be called that. It was more like a cluster of rooms on the ground floor that his family had taken over.

He pulled out a bent key, twisted it in the lock and shoved open a broken door that grated across the concrete floor. "You can hang your jacket on one of the pegs," he said, looking at the blond boy and his flimsy clothing.

"Thanks, but I'll keep it on for now." The boy blew between his cupped hands and rubbed them together.

"You'll soon warm up. There's a fire inside. So, what's your name?" Keir asked while he removed his long gray coat and hat.

"Matt. Matt Hammond."

"I'm Keir Logan. Come in and meet Ma and my sisters, Bronya and Nadia." He removed several potatoes from each coat pocket, then led Matt past several empty rooms and into the kitchen at the end of the corridor. His mother greeted him with a look of complete relief.

"Keir, at last! I was so worried."

"Sorry, Ma. I lost track of time." He kissed his mother on the cheek as always and presented her with the potatoes. Her eyes lit up. She looked so thin these days, often going without food so that everyone else could eat. He felt guilty about bringing home another mouth to be fed. But what was he to do? He couldn't have left anyone to the Gulden Guards. "I've brought someone with me. This is Matt Hammond. Hope you don't mind, Ma. Have you enough for one more?"

His mother smiled. "Sure. I can always squeeze another bowl out of the pot. Come in, boy, and warm yourself by the fire." She turned her head away and coughed. Keir grimaced. Her coughs always sounded so painful.

"Thanks," said Matt. "I don't know where my friends are and I don't have anywhere to go until I find them."

Keir bent in front of the leaping flames, unable to look Matt in the eyes as he broke the news. "I'm sorry to tell you this, but the old man you spoke of was arrested by the Gulden Guards on curfew patrol."

"Gulden Guards?"

"You won't see him again."

"I won't? Why?"

Keir looked up and saw Matt's horrified expression. It was obvious that he really didn't know anything about the curfew patrol. How could he begin to tell him the truth?

His mother came to the rescue. "Keir, go and get your sisters—they're out back stacking firewood. Let's eat first and you can explain to Matt about the horrors of life in Javeer after dinner."

"Javeer?" said Matt. "The *Colony* of Javeer?"

"Yes, this is the Colony of Javeer," replied Keir, bewildered. His new friend paled and shook visibly.

"Then I guess I *won't* be going home for while. I'm meant to be here." Matt paused and swallowed hard. "This must be Level 4."

"Level what?" asked Keir, now totally confused.

"Your Ma's right—let's eat first," said Matt, his voice quaking. "I think this will take a lot of explaining."

Keir shrugged and headed for the back door. "Fine by me—we've got all night. I'll get Bronya and Nadia." He glanced back at his new friend as he pressed down on the handle. No winter clothes . . . Level 4? This was some strange kid. What a night it had turned out to be!

* * * * *

Varl sat cross-legged on the stone floor of the dank jail cell, studying the nine other male inhabitants. He could see them easily in the flickering light of the oil lamps. Each man looked back at him with sunken eyes as though his world had come to an end. Every one of them had refused to answer his questions.

How he longed for a shower. In the three hours he'd been here his hands had turned black, dirt had collected under his nails, and he wondered if he would ever again get a comb through his fine gray hair.

He shuddered at the squalid conditions. Just one small toilet stood in the corner. The hot sticky stench that hung in the air made Varl instantly think of sweat and disease. There was nothing he wouldn't do for one long breath of fresh air and a kind word.

"What's your name?" he asked a middle-aged man sat next to him, for the third time. "I'm Varl."

"Give it a rest, will ya?" the man finally replied. "Stop asking so many questions. A name don't mean nothing in here. You don't wanna get attached to no one, cuz you won't be seeing any of these folk again."

"Where is this place?" Varl pressed.

"Javeer or Boro. Take your pick," he responded with a grunt, and then got up and moved to the other side of the cell.

"Javeer," muttered Varl. "Where have I heard that before?"

The thump of hefty boots approaching caused Varl to turn his attention to the central corridor. A guard appeared at the bars carrying a dirty tray heaped with thick slices of bread. His braided hair was tied back in a long ponytail, and a collection of heavy gold chains hung around his neck over his black leather jacket. Two large golden hoop earrings swung from side to side as he bent to open a small gate near the floor. He slid the tray into the cell and stood up.

Varl sat back as the others dived for the food, fighting over the last crumbs as if they hadn't seen a meal in weeks. The guard was watching too, a hint of amusement in his eyes.

"I demand to see the person in charge," Varl said, scrambling to his feet. He grabbed the bars and looked his jailer in the face. "Please?" he added as an afterthought.

The guard spat on the floor, hitched up his black britches and walked away without a word.

"I insist that you let me go!" Varl shouted, as the guard disappeared through the door at the end of the corridor.

"It's no use asking anything of them." A boy, probably in his mid teens, with olive skin, huge dark eyes and short, tightly curled hair, shouted across the cell. "The Gulden Guards won't answer your questions. They only speak to prisoners when they have to."

Varl wasn't surprised by this revelation. In the whole time he'd been here not one of the guards had uttered more than a grunt. He walked over and sat on the floor next to the boy. Hesitantly he said, "I'm Varl."

"Varl what?"

"Just Varl."

The youth pulled a face and thought for a moment before answering. "I'm Sarven . . . Sarven Morsova."

At last someone was speaking to him! "Pleased to talk to you, Sarven. No one else in here will tell me anything."

"They're just scared, and I don't blame them," Sarven said, swallowing the last words as he ate hungrily.

"What else do you know about the Gulden Guards?"

"Everything . . . but nothing you'll want to hear." He ripped off another huge chunk of bread and stuffed it into his mouth. "Anyway, how come *you* don't know anything about them?"

"I'm not from here. I was just passing through when I

suddenly got arrested."

Sarven sighed deeply. "Shame. You were in the wrong place at the wrong time. You're in a heap of trouble, you know."

"I worked that out," said Varl. "But I've no idea what I was arrested for."

Sarven's eyes narrowed as if he were weighing up Varl. "I'll tell you that and a lot more, but it will cost you."

Varl shook his head in disbelief. "I've nothing to give you but the clothes I'm wearing."

Sarven laughed. "Material things won't do me any good down here. I'm looking for protection and survival."

"Protection? I'm an old man. I don't know what kind of protection you think you'll get from me."

"We'll do better working together—looking out for each other, if you know what I mean."

Varl nodded. "Okay. I can see the benefits of that partnership."

"Right. And I want some of your daily bread rations too."

Varl shrugged. "I don't eat much anyway."

Sarven reached out and shook Varl's hand firmly. "Deal?"

"Deal," said Varl.

The boy moved closer. "There's a 9:00 curfew in the Dark End of Javeer, and you broke it, old man."

"I seem to remember hearing a clock chime," said Varl.

"Right. That was the curfew bell you heard, not a

clock. Twice every night it sounds. The first time, at 8:55 is just a warning to be on your way home. The second time the bell tolls, you must be home—if you're not and you're caught . . . well . . . you end up here in Central Jail."

"How many days will they keep us locked up?" asked Varl.

Sarven gave a hollow laugh. He looked at Varl sideways for a few seconds. "Days? This'll be a shock, so best prepare yourself."

Varl frowned. "It can't be that bad, surely. All I did was break the curfew."

Suddenly the teenager's face turned grim. A muscle quivered at his jaw. "You'll never see daylight again. None of us will."

"What . . . because I broke the curfew?" said Varl, raising his voice.

"Uh-huh. There's been a lot of trouble here since Javeer took over Boro."

"Boro?"

Sarven swallowed hard. "This was the Republic of Boro until nineteen years ago when Horando Javeer marched in from Redinia with his Gulden Guards. He killed everyone who held a seat in our congress, and anyone else who opposed him. Then he claimed Boro as his colony and renamed it Javeer. Two weeks later he proclaimed himself Keeper of the Colony. So now this is the Colony of Javeer with a tyrant for a ruler, instead of the Republic of Boro with a democratic government. Most people still call this place Boro in their own homes. There were riots in the streets, murders and looting, and the worst of it was in the Dark End."

"And that's why there's a curfew in the Dark End."

"Uh-huh. But there's also a curfew in other parts of the colony that have refused to accept Javeer's rule. The penalty for breaking the curfew is harsh because of all the trouble."

"So we're going to be held prisoner indefinitely?"

He lowered his head. "Nope," he said softly. "Much worse."

"Worse?" Varl nearly choked on the word. "What's worse than that?"

Sarven looked up at Varl. He gritted his teeth and said slowly, "The mines, old man."

"What kind of mines?"

The boy moved in close. "Gold . . . gold mines. And we'll soon be mining the gold for Horando Javeer."

Varl sighed and tipped his head back against the bars of the cell. "I'm way too old for that."

"Yeah, right. And I'm too young for that! Anyway, you don't have a choice. There's nobody that likes mining, 'specially as lots of people have died down there."

"Mining has never been safe. Even with modern equipment it is a dangerous profession."

Sarven grimaced. "I'm not talking about people getting killed in cave-ins or from the heat or breathing in the dust."

"So what are you talking about?" Varl pressed.

Fear, stark and vivid, glimmered in Sarven's eyes. "The gold's very deep—over two miles down. If you ask me, that's deeper than humans were ever meant to go. What I meant is . . . well . . . there are monsters down there—things called Gnashers!"

Varl looked at the boy's wide brown eyes and horrorstruck face. "Are you sure the guards aren't just trying to scare you?"

Sarven puckered up his lips, obviously annoyed by Varl's tone. "I've seen the proof."

"What proof?"

"The dead bodies. Gulden Guards are sent home to Redinia every month to be buried. They're completely covered in tiny teeth marks. I saw them loading the bodies onto the gunships."

Varl laughed. "I'm a scientist. There could be a scientific explanation for what you've seen. Have you actually seen a Gnasher?"

Sarven's eyes narrowed. He gave Varl an angry, indignant look. "No. But what else would put those bite marks in the guards? You'll not be laughing when the Gnashers get you!"

Varl searched his face for the truth. Had Sarven really witnessed such horrors or was he just trying to frighten him for some reason? He'd only known the boy for a few hours—not long enough to know what kind of kid was behind the huge dark eyes. Varl's stomach churned. His adventures with Matt should have taught him that the stories could be true. After all, he'd just finished dealing with eight-foot venom-spitting lizards called Vorgs. Perhaps Gnashers really did inhabit the mines of Javeer!

Chapter 2

Targon stood by the door of the wood-paneled study watching Matt's mother walk across the dining room and back to the kitchen. He hovered on the threshold, wondering if he should follow her. What was he doing in Matt's house and why hadn't he returned home to Zaul as Matt had promised?

"Matt should be standing here—not me!" he muttered angrily.

And where *was* Matt? This computer-game thing was just ridiculous. He wished that he'd never set eyes on Matt or his stupid laptop.

Targon looked down at the sling on his arm and remembered his narrow escape from the Vorgs. His shoulder felt better so he removed the sling and threw it on the floor. What should he do now?

He turned and saw there was another computer in the corner of the study. It purred quietly, and brightly colored lines swirled across the dark screen. He'd never seen anything like that on Matt's laptop before. Where were the pictures of Cybergon Protectors marching across the screen or alien Vorgs entering their spacecraft? Without Matt to play his game, Targon had no clue what he should do or how he would ever find his way back to Zaul. One thing was for sure—he couldn't just stand in Matt's study forever. He edged toward the computer. If he touched the keys would Matt then appear? He instantly recognized the '*Enter*' key. Should he try pressing it as he had seen Matt do so many times? He lifted his finger above the key . . .

"Seen Matt?" came a voice from behind him.

Targon jumped and sprang back from the computer, feeling as though he'd been caught doing something that he shouldn't. He whirled around to see a tall blond teenager swing from the doorframe into the study.

"Er . . . no . . . sorry, I haven't seen him," said Targon. He smiled weakly at the older boy, who towered over him. "I was hoping *you* might have."

The boy looked confused. "Nope."

"I think he went to . . . um . . . find his instruction manual . . . ages ago," added Targon.

"Well, he's not in his room. Say, I've not seen you in school. You new around here?"

Targon nodded. "Sort of," was all he could think to say.

"I'm Jake . . . Matt's brother."

"Oh, hi. I'm Targon."

Apart from the blond hair, Jake looked nothing like Matt. His bulbous nose dominated his long face. And why did he have those gleaming metal bands attached to his teeth? Targon found himself staring at Jake's dazzling mouth every time he spoke.

"Okay . . . Targon . . . When Matt gets back from

wherever, tell him to return my new games *right* now. I'm missing two. I'll bet anything he's got 'em somewhere and I'm getting madder by the minute."

"Is *Keeper of the Kingdom* yours, then? Matt said it was a new game."

Jake frowned. "Keeper of the what?"

"Kingdom . . . *Keeper of the Kingdom*. Matt started playing when . . ." Targon stopped in mid-sentence. He felt a lump rise up in his throat. Would Jake believe him if he said that Matt had been pulled into the game?

Jake didn't seem to register Targon's last comment. He pushed him roughly to one side and plunked himself in front of the computer screen.

"New game, eh? Don't remember him getting this," he said, a puzzled expression on his face. He tapped a few keys.

Targon shrugged. "He's already beaten the first three levels."

Jake's thick blond eyebrows shot up in the air. "Really? Well, I'll tell you something, if kid brother's on Level 4 it can't be that difficult." He laughed loudly.

"Seems pretty hard to me," said Targon. He watched Jake easily access the main Menu and pull up the rules as Matt had done so often. Targon thought for a moment. He felt a wave of exhilaration as a plan formed in his mind. "I'll bet you can't complete Level 4 before he gets back," he said in a teasing tone.

"You've gotta be joking," Jake laughed.

"No, I wasn't," said Targon, studying Jake's face to

see if he might rise to the challenge. "Matt says he can beat you any day of the week!"

Jake snorted. "Did he, now? That's just a load of talk. Matt's all talk. I'll show that dork, and I've got you as a witness." He gestured to the far side of the room with his head. "Pull up the chair and fill me in on the rules. I'll be done before he gets back—no sweat."

Targon smiled to himself as he dragged the chair across the room. Matt always said he was full of good ideas. "You've done it again, Targon," he would say. If Matt wasn't here to play the game and get him home to Zaul, then perhaps Jake could do it instead.

*　*　*　*　*

Matt sat crossed-legged on an uncomfortable rush mat in front of the blazing fire. His spirits sank as he watched Keir restlessly move the burning logs around in the fireplace with a long metal poker. During dinner, he'd suddenly realized that he hadn't seen his laptop since he arrived in Javeer, and he'd been agonizing about it ever since. What had happened to it? He hoped that it was somewhere close by. But in any case, he had a whole load of problems to sort out before he could even start Level 4 of his computer game.

At least he was warm and his stomach was somewhat satisfied. The soup had been delicious. He would have liked more, but he'd been all too aware of the small portions around the table, and had quickly realized that there was no such thing as leftovers in this family.

Bronya sat down next to him. Matt watched her huge dark eyes twinkle in the glow from the fire. He'd found her fascinating from the instant she'd walked into the room. Her black hair was roughly cut around her almost perfectly oval face, as though her mother had tried, but failed, to style it into a neat bob. She was bright and intelligent, and had monopolized the conversation throughout dinner. Nadia, on the other hand, was several years younger and more serious. Although also attractive, with dark eyes and dark hair like her older sister, she was quiet spoken and painfully shy.

"Now that we've eaten, tell us where you're from and what you're doing here," Bronya said excitedly. "Have you traveled a long way?"

Keir put down the poker, sat on the hearth, and focused his attention on Matt.

Matt winced. He had been stupidly hoping this question would never come. He looked at the expectant faces. Even Mrs. Logan and Nadia had stopped washing pots to hear what he had to say. This would be difficult, especially as he knew so little about Javeer. What should he use as his excuse this time? Would time travel be acceptable as an answer yet again?

He looked around at the sparse furniture and crude surroundings. Oil lamps provided lighting, and the running water in the sink was cold. There were signs that electrical outlets had once been in the walls, but he hadn't seen so much as a radio. When had technology last been in Javeer? And how sophisticated had that technology been?

Would Keir and his family even understand what a computer was?

What could he tell them? He cleared his throat several times, stalling while he searched for the right answer. The Govans in Level 3 of his game had talked often about the neighboring Colony of Javeer. It was worth a try. He prayed that Keir's family had also heard of the Empire of Gova. That explanation might do for now.

Matt drew in a deep breath. "I've just come from Gova. You've probably heard about the Vorgs taking over the Govan Empire?" he said with a shaky voice.

"Of course," Bronya responded instantly. "Word spreads fast. The Govans were helping us fight Horando Javeer and his Gulden Guards until those horrible lizard-like beasts invaded Gova. Those poor people."

Matt sighed with relief and relaxed a little. His story had worked. "The Vorgs weren't easy to beat. It took some doing, but I found their weakness—and they're gone for good," he said more confidently.

Keir sprang to his feet with a look of sheer delight on his wind-burned face. "I knew it! *You're* the one we've been waiting for!"

"I am?"

Bronya's eyes widened. "Of course! Now I remember. The Govan Resistance said they were sending someone."

"They did?" asked Matt, wondering what he'd said to trigger that assumption. Indeed he *had* worked with the Resistance in Gova to destroy the Vorgs, but they certainly hadn't sent him to Javeer.

"You're the runner from Gova!" said Keir, ignoring Matt's questioning tone and patting him heavily on the back. "Now I understand why you said you were meant to be here and you wouldn't be going home for a while. Welcome, my friend, welcome."

Matt hoped his total confusion didn't show. He smiled and tried to cover up the fact that he had no idea what Keir was talking about. Runner? What was that? At least Keir had accepted his story, even if he'd made some incorrect assumptions about why Matt was here in Javeer.

"We've been waiting for you for months," continued Keir. "The Govans promised to send someone to help our Underground find Horando's weakness, but when the Vorgs arrived in Gova we gave up hope. Now here you are. *You* found the Vorgs' weakness and so they've sent you to help us."

"The Underground?" Matt questioned.

"Our network of people across the colony who are preparing a rebellion," Keir explained. "It's like your Resistance in Gova. I'm proud to be one of them. I'm also a runner, like you. That's what I was doing out tonight—bringing back information from the North End of Javeer. Tomorrow I'll relay that information to the Dark End Underground Council."

Mrs. Logan shook her head. "And I'm terrified every time you go out that door," she said, stopping to cough. "I worry that I'll never see you again."

Keir turned to his mother, who had walked over to listen. "Ma, I know you're worried about me, but someone has to stand up to Horando Javeer. While he's in power, there's no future for any of us. We're prisoners, poor and starving. We can't go on living like this. Look at you, Ma!"

Mrs. Logan began to cough so violently that she had to turn away. "I'm sorry. I'm not feeling well," she said hoarsely. "I should go to bed. Matt, I hope you'll stay with us as long as you need to. We haven't much furniture, but we've plenty of blankets."

"Thank you, Mrs. Logan, you're very kind," said Matt. "And the food was great."

She smiled and touched him on the shoulder. "I'm thankful that you're here to help us, but I hope you know what you're doing, young man. Keir seems to think this is some kind of exciting game. He seems to forget that the Gulden Guards are very real and the consequences of being caught are fatal."

Matt couldn't help but smile at the mention of a game. "Don't worry, Mrs. Logan, you'll be rid of Horando Javeer in a few weeks, I promise. I've dealt with his kind before. We'll find a way to play Horando Javeer at his own game and we'll beat him, you'll see."

"I hope so. I really hope so," she muttered, coughing again as she left the room.

Matt shuddered at his bravado. Why had he said all that? He felt for these people and their frugal existence, but he'd gotten carried away by the moment. He bit his lip wondering why he'd given her so much cause for optimism. The first three levels of his computer game had not been easy and Level 4 of *Keeper of the Kingdom* would be even more of a challenge. He didn't know a thing about Horando Javeer and the Gulden Guards, and without his computer he had no way to begin. Why had he got himself involved with the Logan family's problems when he had so many of his own to take care of first? Where were Varl and Targon? And where was his laptop?

He sighed. This was not a good start to Level 4 of his computer game!

"Ma's pretty sick," whispered Bronya as her mother left the room. "We're very worried about her."

Keir waited for the door to close behind their mother, and then beckoned Nadia to join them by the fire. His face was radiant. Matt could see the hope and excitement in his eyes.

"So, Matt Hammond, where will you begin?" Bronya asked.

Matt was at a loss for words. He *couldn't* begin—not unless he found his computer.

"You said something about Level 4 before dinner. What's that?" asked Keir.

"Umm . . . well . . . Level 4 is a code for how difficult the situation is," Matt replied, fumbling his way through an explanation and regretting that he had ever mentioned Level 4. "We classified the Empire of Gova, and the problem they had with the Vorgs, as a Level 3 situation. We think that your situation is worse."

"Really?" questioned Bronya. "Worse than the Vorgs?"

Matt nodded. "Worse than the Vorgs. So we've classified this as a Level 4."

"You keep saying *we*," said Keir. "Who's we? And who thinks our situation is worse than the Vorgs?"

Matt drew in a deep breath. His heart pumped furiously. Now he had *really* got himself in a fix. How was he going to get out of this one? "I'm not *exactly* part of the Govan Resistance and I'm not originally from Gova."

"You're not?" replied Keir and Bronya in unison, their expressions changing from smiles to looks of confusion.

"Then why did you say you had come from Gova?" asked Keir angrily.

"I said I had *just* come from Gova. It is where I was living last. I helped the Govans get rid of the Vorgs and I've now been sent here to help you get rid of Horando Javeer."

Keir looked relieved. "Whew! You had me worried for a minute. So you are a runner, then."

Matt smiled, unsure of how to answer. "You could call me that, I guess."

"But who sent you if it wasn't the Govans?" asked Bronya.

"I'm from a country called the United States of America and I belong to a much bigger organization . . . called . . . umm . . . the Sons of Liberty," said Matt, thinking quickly and remembering his eighth-grade U.S. history class. "The Sons of Liberty free people all over the Earth in 2540 from their oppressors."

"Oppressors?" asked Nadia. "What are they?"

"An oppressor is a tyrant," explained Matt. "Someone who abuses their power and rules unjustly."

"In other words, Horando Javeer," Bronya cut in.

"Exactly. I brought two other people from the Sons of Liberty to help us, but I don't know what has happened to either of them."

"You're talking about the old man that was taken by the Gulden Guards and the boy you asked me about," said Keir.

Matt nodded. "Varl, a brilliant scientist, and Targon, a friend of mine. We'll need them both if we want to go up against Javeer. They come up with great solutions to problems and we work well together as a team."

"Varl and Targon," said Bronya. "We'll start looking for them tomorrow."

Keir began to pace in front of the fire. "I might be able to find out what happened to the old man," he said enthusiastically. "It'll be risky, but I have my contacts in the Underground. I suspect Varl is in Central Jail, but someone will know for sure."

Matt hesitated and then added, "There's another problem. I'm missing a vital piece of equipment—my laptop, which is a small computer. All of the information I had collected about Javeer and the Gulden Guards is stored on my laptop. I must have dropped it when we bumped into each other tonight in the dark."

"Then we'll find that, too," said Bronya, her expression determined. "I don't know what a lap thing is, but if you describe it to me, it shouldn't be too difficult to find."

"Laptop computer," corrected Matt.

Bronya smiled. "Laptop computer. We'll have to wait

until morning when the curfew is lifted, of course. Nadia and I will retrace your steps. I'm sure we'll find it."

"*Then* we'll be able to get to work," said Keir, rubbing his hands together. "The sooner we're rid of Horando Javeer, the better!"

Matt smiled weakly at his three new friends. He had survived the Logan family's interrogation and won their trust, in spite of making up some far-fetched story about the Sons of Liberty.

He stared into the roaring flames, comforted by the warmth from the glowing logs. The next few days would be a real challenge. Without his computer he could do little to help them or even start Level 4 of his game.

"Zang it!" he muttered. Where could his laptop be this time?

* * * * *

Varl awoke to the sound of jingling keys and the clanging of jail doors being opened. As he tried to sit up he grimaced. At his age he was not meant to sleep on a hard concrete floor. He twisted his neck from side to side and rubbed the small of his back to relieve the stiffness.

"Get up, old man, quick!" whispered Sarven. "The guards are entering the cell."

Varl scrambled to his feet as fast as his old bones would allow. He had barely stood up when something swished past his face, catching his hair and making the sound of a loud smack. Instantly he realized it was a whip.

A guard stood in front of him, face twisted into a smirk. "Out!" he hollered, snapping the whip in front of Varl's face a second time. Varl flinched.

He followed Sarven into the corridor and joined the line that was forming. At least ten Gulden Guards stood watch, all dressed in black knee-length pants and matching leather jackets draped with gold necklaces.

"You have all been sentenced to two years in the mine," announced one of the guards.

"Could have been worse," muttered Sarven.

Across the corridor, prisoners pressed their faces between the cell bars, staring at Varl and Sarven. "Good luck, my friends," one of them whispered, reaching out to touch Varl's hand as the line moved toward the door.

Varl's heart raced. Was there nothing they could do? He quickly counted the prisoners. He guessed that there were around thirty people, mostly men of all ages, from young teens to men older than himself. There were at least twenty guards, each armed with a whip and a golden gun that hung from a heavily studded black belt.

"What are the weapons?" he whispered to Sarven.

"ST29s. You get hit with one of them and you'll not get up again. They propel you twenty feet in the air without making a sound! That's why the Gulden Guards carry whips as well. The ST29s are a last resort."

Varl winced. The Gulden Guards would easily overpower this group and probably wouldn't hesitate to kill. He had no choice but to do as he was told and go with the others.

Varl followed the line through the door and into a brightly lit room. He squinted while his eyes adjusted to the light. It was then that he noticed that everyone else wore thick winter clothing while he had only thin baggy blue pants and a short-sleeved top. Would they be going outside into the freezing weather?

He quickly found out. A guard opened the outer door and an icy wind whipped into the room. Varl peered into the street and saw that several inches of snow had fallen overnight. He shuddered and instantly wrapped his arms around himself in an effort to keep warm.

The line inched forward out into the biting cold and toward a huge waiting aircraft, its engines already roaring.

Varl shuffled carefully in the snow, fighting to put one foot in front of the other as he battled up the slippery steps of the aircraft in the whipping wind. He used the handrail, determined to get inside as fast as he could.

"Not good. This is not good," muttered Sarven as they sat down on the freezing metal floor with the other prisoners. "We've boarded a gunship."

"You think we're being taken to the mine already?" whispered Varl.

Sarven nodded. "Uh-huh. That's my guess. It's only a short flight."

"Some good news, then," said Varl sarcastically. He was chilled to the bone from his few minutes outside. Sitting on the cold floor of the gunship made him feel even worse.

"I hope we're given lighter clothing when we get there," Sarven muttered.

Varl massaged his legs to keep the circulation going. "Why? Right now I'd give anything for what you're wearing."

"You'll not be saying that when we're below ground. I've been told that the temperature can reach more than 140 degrees in the mine."

"Can that be true—140 degrees?" said Varl in a horrified whisper. "How can anyone be expected to survive in that kind of heat?"

Sarven shrugged. "Beats me—but that's a known fact. I guess that's why so many die in the mines . . . that and malnutrition. I've heard they don't feed you much."

The gunship's doors closed, shutting out the icy wind, but with the only light coming from the cockpit windows, it was almost dark in the belly of the metal giant. Everyone fell silent as the roar of the engines increased, and with a slight judder the craft lifted into the air. Varl felt relieved. At least he was warmer.

He grabbed Sarven's arm to steady himself as the gunship tilted first to the right and then to the left. He could just make out Sarven's silhouette in the low light. His long thin nose and slightly pointed chin reminded him of Matt. Where was his young friend? And what had happened to Targon? Had the Gulden Guards also captured them?

Varl tried to clear his mind. What was the use of worrying about the boys if he could do nothing to help them anyway? He felt sure that this was another level of Matt's computer game, and that this one had something to do with Horando Javeer and the Gulden Guards. He'd learn all he could about them so that *when* he met up with Matt again, he could help him solve the riddle and locate the Keeper. Varl was determined that he would be ready. But for now, he had only one thought. How was he going to stay alive?

Chapter 3

"What's Matt's password?" asked Jake, hands poised above the keyboard. "I can't access his saved game and get straight to Level 4 without it."

"Oh, right." *Think, Targon. Think back to when Matt first opened his game. What did he tell you?* If he couldn't remember Matt's password, they wouldn't be able to play, and his plan would fail. Targon had a sinking feeling in the pit of his stomach. He hadn't paid attention to what Matt had typed. All he'd seen was a row of large black dots. "Sorry, I have no idea," he replied, feeling utterly miserable.

"No problem," said Jake. "He's a dork, anyway. I've seen him use *Matt1* over and over again. I'll bet you anything he's *still* using it."

Targon didn't reply, annoyed that Jake had called Matt a dork. But he hoped that Jake was right about the password.

"Here we are . . . told you so . . . Keeper of the Colony, Level 4 of *Keeper of the Kingdom*," said Jake. "The dimwit. Couldn't he think of anything more original? You'd better tell him when he gets back that if he wants to keep people out of his business, he's got to think of something better than *Matt1* for a password."

"I'll tell him," muttered Targon.

"So, fill me in on the rules."

"You have to locate the Keeper and free the people to win each level," said Targon. "There are riddles you'll have to solve and you'll be told what to do with the Keeper when you find him."

"How do you mean?" said Jake, turning to look at Targon.

Targon sat up in his chair. He felt knowledgeable even if he still struggled to read some of the instructions on the screen. "Well, in Level 1, we had to destroy the Keeper, in Level 2 we had to deactivate the Keeper, and in the last level we had to activate the Keeper."

"Right," said Jake, kicking back in the swivel chair with his arms folded behind his head. "You said *we*. You've played all the levels with Matt, have you?"

"Sort of," said Targon, not knowing how to respond. "I helped." He wasn't about to say that he was a character *in* Matt's new computer game. Jake would never believe that! Targon hardly believed it himself. If he was just a character, why was he here in Matt's study and not inside the game? Now he didn't know what to believe. Perhaps Varl had been right all along and Matt was really a time traveler. If that were the case, had he now traveled *back* to Matt's time?

"Hey, you listening to me, kid?" bellowed Jake. "I asked you, who or what is the Keeper?"

"Sorry, I was thinking about something else."

"Well, let's get on with it. Matt'll be back any minute."

"Okay. The Keeper," said Targon, pausing to think how best to explain. "The Keeper is always in control and is usually a computer or computer program of some kind. The Keeper is not necessarily the enemy, but could be a program used by the enemy."

"Really," said Jake, frowning so that his eyebrows drew together in the middle for a few seconds.

Targon wondered if Jake really did understand. "You'll see once we start."

"Let's access the first challenge," said Jake.

Targon winced as Jake clicked on *'Rules.'* What pictures and music would greet him this time?

Zigzagging across the screen was a huge lumbering aircraft, its propellers rotating above its giant body. The deafening roar of the engines almost drowned out the soft voice announcing,

"Welcome, players of *Keeper of the Kingdom*. You are entering Level 4, *Keeper of the Colony*. You are about to navigate the Colony of Javeer on expert difficulty. Do you wish to continue with your most daring challenge yet?"

"Click 'yes,'" urged Targon.

"But of course." Jake glared at him in annoyance and moved the mouse accordingly.

The soft computerized voice continued. "Horando Javeer and his Gulden Guards have taken over the Republic of Boro and renamed it the Colony of Javeer, enslaving the people and stealing their wealth. Your task is to locate and destroy the Keeper and free the people of

Boro."

"Well, that's pretty straightforward," said Jake. "What now?"

"Now we have to find out who'll help us in Level 4."

Jake groaned. "Hey, kid. Give me a break and save me time. Which number?"

"Matt always clicked on Number 3 or Number 4. It'll say Liberators or something."

"Nothing like that here," said Jake.

"Are you sure?"

"Number 4 says *'Runner'* and 3 says *'Underground.'*"

"Strange," said Targon. "It's always been something like Liberators or Freedom Fighters before. I'm sure that Matt started with Number 3 last time."

"Hang on," said Jake, breaking into a wide grin for the first time. "Now I'm the dork. The Underground was an organization in World War II. Its members worked secretly against the Nazis. It's the same kind of thing as Liberators."

"Try it then," said Targon eagerly.

Jake clicked on Number 3, *'Underground'* and pressed *'Enter.'*

An eerie foggy landscape dominated the screen. In the dark streets, Targon could make out tall buildings with smashed windows. The toll of a deep bell and the sound of a foghorn added to the sinister scene.

"The Dark End of Javeer," said Jake, reading the top of the screen. "Creepy."

Targon shuddered. "I agree." He thought of Matt and

Varl. Deep down he had a gnawing feeling that they were close by. He stared at the picture. "Hope they're not there," he muttered.

"Who?" said Jake.

"Nothing," said Targon quickly. "Get ready for the riddle. You'll need to save it. Matt always said he saved it as something called a Word document so that he could look at it again later."

Jake gave Targon a strange sideways look. "Duh!" he said. "What else did you think I would do?"

Targon felt his cheeks flush. He had to be careful and remember that he was now in the year 2110—Matt's own time period. Jake would be familiar with expressions and phrases that Matt used.

"Here's the rhyme."

"Read it aloud," said Targon.

"Read it yourself," retorted Jake.

"I'm not a very good reader," said Targon quietly.

"Oh. No problem then," grunted Jake in a sympathetic tone that Targon wasn't expecting. "Neither am I. You ready?"

Targon settled into his chair. "Okay, ready."

Level 4: two players this time
Both must win to end the line.
For help find the underground
But opposition will be found
Those whom you intend to save
Will not be easy to persuade

Your plans are seen as a threat
To destroy their network—not protect.

Do you want a game for one or two players?

"Two, press two players quickly," shouted Targon.

"Give me a chance!" snapped Jake, clicking on *'two players.'* "That's strange . . ."

He pressed on *'two players'* again.

"What? What's strange?"

"I swear I clicked on *'two players.'*"

"You did. I just watched you," said Targon, confident that he could now tell the difference between the words *two* and *one.*

"So why is the level now set up for only one player?"

Targon leaped out of his seat. "But we've got to play with two players," he said. "The rhyme told us that, and whatever the rhyme tells us, we have to do to win!"

Jake yawned and tipped back in the chair. "Beats me—but we're definitely playing together as one player now. I'll bet that's what the rhyme meant—that two players had to team up together."

Targon's heart raced. "You think?"

He sat back down and stared at the black screen, waiting for something to happen. Was Jake right? Or had they lost the fourth level before they'd even started because somehow they hadn't followed directions properly? "Matt would know if we're doing this right," muttered Targon.

"Well, *he* isn't here, and I am," growled Jake, giving Targon a sideways glance. "I'm much better at games, anyway. So quit whining and let's play the game."

Targon bit his lip. Jake was nothing like his gentle younger brother. He studied Jake's determined face and wondered what he had let himself in for. How he wished Matt *were* here!

* * * * *

Bronya threw her long red cape around her shoulders, pulled up the hood and braced herself for the cold wind. She opened the front door and gasped. Over six inches of snow had fallen overnight, temporarily transforming the Dark End into a beautiful, picturesque seaside town.

She looked down at her feet. Her big toe poked through a hole in her left boot and the sole of her right boot had nearly worn through. On any other day new snow would have convinced her to stay at home and keep warm. But today she had a purpose and nothing would prevent her from going outside.

As she stepped into the snow, she could see two sets of footprints leading down the alley. Keir and Matt had set off at dawn to meet with the Dark End Underground Council. If she were careful she might be able to tread in their footprints for a while. It would be easier to walk where the snow had already been trampled.

Nadia came up behind. "Please don't stand with the door open," she chided her sister softly. "We're already low on wood without wasting the heat."

"Sorry," said Bronya. "Are you coming with me?"

Nadia shook her head. "Ma's not doing too well this morning. I'd better stay and keep the fire going."

"I'll see you later, then."

"Be careful, Bron."

Bronya closed the door and battled down the alley against the icy wind. She took some delight in crunching on the freshly fallen snow. The sun glinted off the sparkling surfaces, transforming her normally bleak world.

She turned the corner onto Wharf Street, which was strangely quiet for a Tuesday morning. Usually she would stop at each of the sidewalk stalls to see what food was being sold or bartered. Today it was too cold and no one had set up shop, but she knew that would change by late afternoon when the fishing boats came in. Her stomach rumbled, reminding her that she hadn't eaten.

The run-down First Bank of Boro, where Keir had said he'd bumped into Matt, was the next building on her right. It had to be where Matt had dropped his laptop computer, she reasoned. But her heart sank as she approached. Snow had blown onto the steps and was piled high against the boarded doors. In all that snow how could she possibly find a thin black box such as Matt had described?

She began to shuffle from side to side as she walked up to the building, kicking away the snow in her path. Her toes were already frozen, and now her thin socks were wet and her legs chilled from her knees down. She knelt in the entrance and felt around in the snow with her bare hands. After several minutes of searching, her fingers numb, she stood up, defeated. "Nothing. It's not here."

She heard arguing across the street and turned to see what the commotion was about. Two boys stood on the steps of the Fisherman's Market Hall. They were pulling a black box back and forth.

"It's mine."

"But I saw it first."

"Give it to me. I picked it up."

"Finders, keepers. It's mine, I say!"

"Take your hands off."

"No, you take yours off!"

Bronya stared at the black box in their hands. That had to be Matt's laptop. Her pulse quickened. Matt had said that his laptop held valuable information, and she would be the one to bring it home.

"Excuse me!" said Bronya, running up behind them.

One of the boys turned to look at her. Suddenly he lost his footing and slipped backward off the icy step, causing the other boy to also lose his balance.

Bronya watched in horror as the box was propelled into the air. "Watch out!" she screamed, diving forward with her arms extended in a desperate attempt to catch the valuable possession. Skidding on the slippery surface, she fell, elbows first, and ended up sprawled across the steps. The heavy computer landed awkwardly on her outstretched arms. She winced with the pain and struggled to her feet, heart pounding, elbows throbbing. It was then that she noticed the thin crack across almost the entire length of the lid. Drat! Would Matt still be able to get the information he needed from it?

"Thanks, girl. I'll have that," shouted one of the boys as he whipped the laptop from her grasp and tore off toward the docks.

"Hey! Come back!" shouted Bronya. "That's mine. I need it."

The other boy, still lying in the snow on the sidewalk behind her, broke into laughter. "Finders, keepers! Finders, keepers!" he chanted.

Bronya's anger rose within her. She stormed over to the red-faced boy and stared down at him. "You idiot!" she screamed, her hands on her hips. "That's something called a computer. The information stored inside it could help us all. The Underground is looking for it."

The boy's eyes narrowed. He stared at her through long strands of straight dark hair that had blown forward over his face. "That right? A computer?"

"Now tell me who that boy was and where I can find him."

The boy swept his hair back with his right hand and got to his feet, not bothering to brush himself down. "What's it worth to ya?"

Bronya felt as though her head was about to explode. "What's it worth? You idiot! It's worth a better life for us all. Now tell me . . . who was your friend?"

The boy shrugged. "I dunno," he said with a grin, backing away from her. "No friend of mine. But if the box is that valuable I'll be sure to find out . . . it'll still cost ya, though."

Bronya sighed. "Okay. Two days of food and two days of wood."

"Nope. Not enough."

Now she was really angry. "Three days then . . . and four if you bring me the computer. That's it," said Bronya through clenched teeth. "I'll be going hungry and cold to give you that. Take it or leave it."

"Okay. Done deal. How do I find you?"

"I live in the abandoned warehouse next to the old candy factory here on Wharf Street. Go up the alley between the buildings and you'll see a green door half-way down."

"What's your name?"

"Bronya Logan. What's yours?"

"Gorbun."

"Gorbun what?"

"None of your business."

"Okay, Gorbun whoever," said Bronya, instantly regretting she'd told him so much about herself. "You've got twelve hours and no more. I'll be waiting to hear from you by nine tonight."

"But that's curfew."

"Then you'd better find me by eight," she said, already walking away.

She watched the boy run toward the docks and then turned toward home, angry with herself. How stupid she'd been! She'd had the box in her hands! She knew what life was like in the Dark End. You couldn't trust anyone. You couldn't turn your back or be off guard for one second. Everyone was looking for something special to trade for extra food or wood. It was all about survival. The boy who'd run off with Matt's computer was only looking out for himself.

She desperately wanted to be a runner like Keir and help to defeat Horando Javeer. But Keir thought that girls shouldn't work for the Underground. "It's too dangerous, Bron," he always said. "It's not work that girls can do. You need your wits about you and plenty of courage and strength."

Bronya kicked the snow as she approached her front door. "Courage and strength," she muttered. "I'll show you, Keir Logan." If only she still had the computer. That would have proved her courage to Keir, and would have shown Matt her ingenuity. Now she would have to tell them what had happened—how she'd had the computer in her hands and then had lost it again. She prayed that Gorbun would bring it to her before Keir and Matt returned home.

Chapter 4

Matt pulled his jacket collar tightly around his neck and kept his head down against the bitter cold as he trudged across the pebble beach after Keir. Seawater lapped against his trainers and the icy spray whipped against his cheeks.

He followed Keir in front of the old seawall and under a rotting pier. The smell of salt and seaweed was almost overwhelming. Some of the planks of wood above were missing and others swung in the wind, held in place by one last nail. Matt ducked to avoid them. This was not what he had anticipated when Keir had promised an introduction to the Dark End Underground Council. Why couldn't they have met somewhere in the town center on such a cold day?

Keir came to a sudden halt by one of the pier's barnacle-covered supporting timbers. He pushed Matt back against the seawall and whispered, "Stay here a minute."

Keir ran down to the water's edge, peered around a pillar in either direction, then sprinted back.

"Okay, we haven't been followed."

"I thought you said the curfew began at nine in the evening," said Matt.

"It does. We have every right to be outside. But Horando knows that people are plotting to get rid of him, and his informants turn in anyone who might be a member of the Underground."

"Turn in?"

"Unfortunately some citizens of Boro are so desperate that they're willing to sell information to Horando Javeer in exchange for food and fuel. You *could* call them traitors, I guess. So, if you're not out fishing or bartering for food in the streets, then you stand out from everyone else and could be arrested."

"Great," said Matt. "So you're telling me that we could be in trouble for just being here."

Keir smiled. "Don't worry. They'll not find us." He pulled out a large gray stone from the seawall and set it on the ground. "Stand back," he said as he pushed his right shoulder against the rocks. A section of stone slowly swung inward, revealing a dark passage behind.

"Let's go," said Keir. "It'll be pitch black when I close the door, so stay against the wall and feel your way forward. You'll come to another door. Wait for me there."

"Haven't you got a flashlight?"

"No batteries," said Keir. "Only oil lamps in these hard times, and it would look rather suspicious to carry an oil lamp through the streets on such a sunny day, don't you think?"

Matt began his journey down the passage, walking quickly while light still came in from outside. Then the seawall door shut, and just as Keir had warned, the tunnel went black. Matt suddenly knew what it would be like to lose his sight. No shadows, no shapes, no lighter shades to guide him, just black—the kind of black that was so still and quiet that it made your heart race.

Within minutes Keir caught up and then took the lead. "Take hold of my belt," he instructed.

Matt felt for his friend's coat and was reassured when his fingers curled around the thick fabric belt. Keir set off at a fast pace, which Matt found hard to maintain in the dark even though he was being led.

"Where's this taking us?"

"Back into the city," Keir shouted back. "It's an old route used by fishermen to bring their daily catch into the basement of the market hall. It was more direct from the boats than dragging cart-loads of fish through the streets. The tunnel was closed decades ago when modern transportation arrived. Most people have forgotten about its existence."

"Modern transportation?" asked Matt. He hadn't seen any signs of cars or trucks.

Keir laughed. "Ironic, isn't it? Before Boro became the Colony of Javeer we had electricity, and vehicles powered by sophisticated engines."

"I saw the electrical outlets in the walls in your house," said Matt. "I wondered what had happened."

"My mother remembers those times—about twenty years ago. All of that is gone. Horando got rid of all transportation so that people couldn't travel except on foot. Because of that, trade with neighboring cities stopped. He closed schools, burned books and banned teachers from the colony. Horando wanted poor uneducated people—people who had no means to rise up against him."

"But poor people can rise up and defeat tyrannical rulers," said Matt with authority. "I've seen it and been part of it." After his experiences with the Cybergons, the Noxerans and the Vorgs in the first three levels of his computer game, how well he knew that.

"I hope you're right," said Keir, stopping abruptly. "Because right now we need all the help we can get."

"Well, you've got my help, and if I can find my two friends I know they'll help too. We'll find a way to make Boro free again."

"Thanks. It means a lot. Well, we're here. In a few seconds we'll be able to see again."

Matt listened in the darkness to the sound of grating rocks. Before long, a narrow band of light shone in his eyes, widening as Keir pushed open the door. Finally Matt could see a large room, and the warmth from within instantly hit him. He eagerly followed Keir inside. However, when he saw three people seated around the blazing fire he hung back, waiting for an introduction.

Keir removed his coat as he entered. "Greetings, Sorcha."

"Glad you made it safely, Keir. You're late. I was getting worried," replied a middle-aged woman with streaked silver hair.

"Never fear, Keir always gets here," he said with a

wink. "Lorcan, Fionn, I hope you are both well. I have brought a special guest."

As the two men swivelled around in their chairs, Matt saw anger in their faces the instant their eyes fell on him. He decided not to wait for further introductions.

"I'm Matt Hammond, and I'm pleased to meet you all. Keir has told me a lot about you." As soon as the words left his mouth, Matt realized that he had said the wrong thing.

"Keir! What are you doing bringing a stranger to this meeting? Are you mad?" Sorcha exploded.

"Not at all. Wait until you hear what Matt has to say."

Sorcha's face darkened. "We will not wait! You're endangering the whole Underground network. You know that runners have to remain secret in case someone is captured. Only the members of the Underground Council know who the runners are, and that is for everyone's safety. *We* do the recruiting of new runners, not you!"

"Sorcha, please, I'm not putting anyone in danger. Matt is *not* from Javeer and he *doesn't* want to be a runner."

One of the men got to his feet, anger evident on his face. "You'd better have a very good explanation, young man."

"But Lorcan . . ." Keir began.

Matt stepped forward before Keir could say another word. "I'm from an organization called the Sons of Liberty."

"Never heard of them," said Sorcha in a scathing tone.

Matt swallowed hard. Convincing the Dark End

Underground Council was not going to be as easy as fooling the Logan family. He ignored her comments and continued. "I'm here with valuable information to help you get rid of Horando Javeer. My last assignment was in Gova where I helped the Govan Resistance get rid of the Vorgs."

"Govan Resistance, eh?" said Lorcan. He bent to whisper to the bald man next to him.

Matt's spirits rose. Now it seemed they were taking an interest. "It was no easy task, but I knew of the Vorgs' weakness and used that to our advantage. Now the people of Gova are free."

Lorcan shoved his hands in his pant pockets and began to pace in a circle around Matt, close enough that Matt could feel his hot breath.

"You realize we can check this information," said Lorcan, coming around to face Matt, his voice calm.

"Of course," Matt quickly replied. "Send a runner to Gova. The Govan Resistance will confirm who I am and that I'm telling you the truth."

"We'll do that immediately," said Sorcha, slamming her hands down on the table. "But in the meantime, you'll remain here in this room as our guest."

"Guest? You mean prisoner!" shouted Keir. "You can't treat someone who has come to help us like this. Matt can stay with me. I'll take responsibility for him."

"Fionn, tie the boy's wrists and ankles!" snapped Sorcha.

The burly balding man who had been silent throughout

the whole discussion quickly got to his feet. Matt felt his chest tighten as Fionn took one of his arms, pulled him across the room, and pushed him into a chair close to the fire. Matt didn't attempt to struggle free. He had to prove that he had no reason to run.

"Please, don't do this," Matt implored as Fionn bound his ankles tightly with rope and then pulled his hands behind the chair. "I'm not a threat. I can help you defeat Horando Javeer."

"I can't believe I'm seeing this!" shouted Keir.

"We can't take any chances," said Sorcha. "You should've thought more carefully before bringing him here. What do you really know of this young man? What proof do you have that Matt Hammond is who he says he is, and not a spy for the Gulden Guards? You were stupid bringing him here, Keir. Now he can identify the members of the Dark End Underground Council and we must cover for your mistake."

Keir fell silent. He looked at Matt with doleful eyes and sighed heavily. "I just know he can be trusted," he said quietly. "You'll regret treating an ally like this."

"Regret? Never!" said Sorcha. "If I have wrongly detained this young man, I can live with my mistake. However, if he were to take back information to Horando and destroyed everything we have worked for, that mistake I could not live with. Until we have proof, I am protecting the people of Boro and our Underground organization. Taking chances could put us all in danger. If he's here to help, we'll find out soon enough."

"Keir, find my laptop, please," said Matt, realizing that he could do nothing to convince them. "I've got a lot of valuable information about Horando Javeer stored in its memory, which will help the Underground and be further proof that I am telling the truth."

"Keir can look for whatever you need—this laptop," said Sorcha. "For now, Matt Hammond, I suggest you make yourself comfortable and enjoy the fire. Lorcan will stay here and keep you company, and we'll send a runner to Gova. I'll be back to check on you tonight. We'll know if you are speaking the truth before tomorrow morning."

"Before morning?" repeated Matt. "I can't wait that long!"

"You can't wait that long? Wait for what?" asked Fionn.

Matt felt his cheeks warm. "Umm . . . I can't wait to make plans. Every hour is vital."

"There's nothing that can't wait for a few hours when we've lived in this situation for years," said Sorcha. "Keir, collect your runner's food reward from the cupboard, and later tonight you can brief us on what you found out."

Matt watched as Sorcha disappeared into the room beyond. Fionn gave Keir a look of disgust and quickly followed.

"I'm sorry," said Keir. "If I'd thought for a moment that they would do this to you, I'd never have brought you along."

"It's okay. I don't like this but I do understand why they're doing it. You've got to find my laptop. It's a black rectangular box about eighteen inches by twelve inches, and about an inch deep. It has a crack across the lid."

Keir turned his back to Lorcan and mouthed, "Maybe Bronya has found it."

Matt nodded and sighed heavily. "If it's not on Wharf Street I don't know where else it might be."

Keir patted Matt on the shoulder. "I've got to get wood for Ma for the night. I'll be back in a few hours."

Matt watched his new friend leave back through the passageway. Matt felt depressed. Once again in this game he was alone and his situation seemed grim. His laptop was missing, he was being held hostage, and he was caught in a web of lies about who he was and why he was here.

"The Sons of Liberty," he muttered angrily. He'd created that organization only the night before, so no one in Gova would have heard of them. He prayed that someone in Gova would at least verify that Matt Hammond had helped to defeat the Vorgs using his computer. It was the best he could hope for. One thing was certain—the next few hours would seem like a lifetime.

* * * * *

Bronya heard a heavy knock on the door.

"I'll get it," she shouted to Nadia and excitedly ran down the hallway. Perhaps it was Gorbun with Matt's computer!

"Who is it?" she asked.

"It's Gorbun."

Her heart fluttered as she unbolted the door. Gorbun stood in front of her, grinning broadly, his hands clasped behind his back.

"Did you find the computer?" she asked.

He nodded, his long hair hiding his eyes.

Bronya felt like dancing. How happy Keir and Matt would be! "That's wonderful news. Give it to me then and our deal will be sealed. I'll keep my part of the bargain—four days of food and firewood for your family, as promised."

"Four days' supply is not enough."

"What do you mean?" Bronya scowled. "I thought we had a deal."

"I got a better one."

Bronya watched with horror as Gorbun stepped to one side and three Gulden Guards appeared from the shadows. They quickly formed a line across her doorway, their ST29s aimed at her.

"Bronya Logan, you are under arrest for plotting against Horando Javeer," said one of the guards. "You'll come with us."

"You rotten rat!" Bronya screamed at Gorbun. "How could you betray me?"

Gorbun shrugged. He looked at his feet and mumbled. "Sorry, but I gotta take care of my family. You understand. Nothin' personal or anythin', but you don't mean diddly-squat to me."

"What about *my* family? Didn't you think about what you'd be doing to them?"

"You're a traitor, so what does it matter?" said Gorbun, turning his head away.

"*I'm* a traitor?" screamed Bronya, as the guards turned her around and roughly tied her hands. "*You're* the traitor! You think about that when you're feeding your fat face!"

"Bron, what's the fuss? What's happening?" asked Nadia, running to the door.

"I've been arrested," said Bronya, fighting back the tears. Her sister's young face seemed to age before her eyes.

"But why? Where are they taking you?"

"Ask that traitor! Ask *him*!" shouted Bronya as the guards dragged her from her house and into the street. "He'll tell you."

Nadia ran behind and grabbed Bronya's skirt. "Stop! Guards! You can't just take her away without an explanation. Tell me what she's accused of."

The guards ignored Nadia's pleas. Bronya heard the fabric of her skirt tear as the guards wrenched her away from her sister and frog-marched her down the alley in the snow. She could hear Nadia sobbing in the distance. Her stomach knotted as her eyes focused on the waiting gunship. A crowd of people had gathered in the middle of Wharf Street. They muttered and gawked at her. She fought back the tears as the guards forced her up the steps of the gunship. What would happen to her now? Would she ever see her family again? How she wished she had never laid eyes on Matt Hammond or his little black computer.

* * * * *

The guards unlocked the huge gunship door and Varl braced himself for the onslaught of the bitter wind. He was already so cold that he couldn't feel his toes. How much more could his old body take?

Varl struggled to stand as a gust of wintry wind blasted through the gunship. When he reached the door he stood in the sunlight for a moment. Even as the wind whipped against his face he looked toward the sun and smiled. He had often taken such simple pleasures for granted. Today, in the bleak weather, nature's warm gift offered him hope of survival.

Sarven took hold of his elbow and together they battled across the icy concrete to a convoy of waiting open-top trucks. Varl climbed uneasily into the back of the first truck and squeezed onto a wooden bench in between a large man in a thick coat and a heavily built Gulden Guard in a black leather jacket. He was thankful that he was sandwiched between two larger men on such a cold day.

Sarven clambered onto the facing bench and gave Varl a half-smile. Varl smiled back, glad for the familiar face of his friend. The engine revved, the truck lurched forward and he prepared himself for a rough ride.

"Okay, old man?" asked Sarven, as the truck's hard suspension jolted them up and down.

"Frozen—but okay," said Varl. "I'm sure my old bones will ache for a day or two after this—if I don't die of pneumonia first."

"Shut your mouths," said one of the guards, waving his coiled whip in a threatening manner.

Varl turned his attention to their route. He knew he must take in every detail of the journey, as it might be useful information later. The trucks traveled through a thick pine forest, then across a snow-covered plain toward craggy peaks. Gone was the sea and the monotonous foghorn, and gone too was the city with its crumbling buildings. Instead, the mountainous landscape stretched for miles. Finally in the distance Varl could see a cluster of buildings surrounded by a tall fence. He wondered if the village was their destination. Against the harsh surroundings it looked quite inviting, he thought.

But as the convoy approached, Varl quickly changed his mind. This was no village—it was a compound. Surrounding the buildings was a fence topped with three feet of barbed wire, and guard towers at least forty feet tall stood on every corner. Outside the main gate a sign, *Horando Gold Mine*, suspended by chains from two wooden posts, squeaked as it swung in the wind.

The convoy stopped at the entrance and several Gulden Guards holding ST29s inspected each truck. The gates opened and the convoy proceeded. Varl's heart sank when he saw two inner electric fences ten feet apart. This was nothing more than a fortified prison surrounded by beautiful mountains.

He looked up. Thick cables that hung from huge steel supports crisscrossed the slushy streets. He could hardly believe what he saw as the truck drove into the main square and past the entrances to the mine. Street signs indicated directions to shafts one, two or three, and in the few minutes it took for them to drive past shaft one, at least five locomotive-driven hoppers filled with blasted rock arrived at the surface. Armed Gulden Guards were positioned around every hopper, watching shivering prisoners unload the rock into waiting trucks.

Varl tried to adjust to the drone of the enormous surface fans and the loud hum of the refrigeration units that drowned out all other street sounds. A steady stream of frail, dirty men and a few women walked from the shafts' elevators toward the low buildings around the perimeter. He presumed those were prisoners' accommodation and that he would soon be assigned a home.

In every direction Varl saw black leather jackets and ST29s. The huge numbers of Gulden Guards sent an immediate message to the new arrivals—escape was not an option. Varl's ray of hope had been quickly dashed. Now he felt nothing but despair.

Chapter 5

Keir trudged down Wharf Street in the snow, boiling with rage. He understood that Sorcha, Fionn and Lorcan were protecting the Underground organization, but why had they been so quick to suspect Matt? Now his new friend was a hostage.

He turned the corner into the alley and heard screaming. As he sprinted toward home he could see that Nadia was holding onto a boy's coat.

"You're not leaving here, Gorbun!" she shouted. "Not 'til you tell me what you told the Gulden Guards."

"What's going on?" asked Keir, fighting for breath. The boy struggled to shake off Nadia's hold. Keir shoved him hard against the alley wall, towering over him. "*You're* not going anywhere. Who are you, anyway?"

"This is Gorbun. He's a good-for-nothing traitor who's just turned Bronya over to the Gulden Guards."

"You did what?" roared Keir, pushing hard against the boy's chest.

"I turned her in for consorting with the enemy," replied Gorbun matter-of-factly. He raised his hands meekly above his head and tried to walk away.

"Consorting with the enemy?" yelled Keir, grabbing the boy's arms and swinging him back against the wall a second time.

Gorbun puffed out his chest and stood upright as if he were trying to look bigger. "She wanted this black thing I found. Told me that it contained secrets that would be useful to the Underground. I just passed the information on, that's all."

"That's all?" said Keir, anger rising in his voice. "Because my sister *mentioned* the word Underground you sold her out to Horando Javeer without a thought. She's not a member of the Underground. She doesn't know where to find them or anything about them. You sold her out because it suited you."

"Look, I gotta take care of my family. You know the score. The Gulden Guards gave me a month's supply of wood and food. There isn't anyone in the Dark End who's gonna turn down that kind of a deal."

It took all of Keir's self-control to stop himself from wrapping his hands around the boy's throat. "Oh yes there is. There are plenty of honorable people who wouldn't rat out their friends. Plenty who are working hard to stay alive and find a way to regain control of Boro."

Gorbun brushed his long hair away from his eyes. "Bronya Logan's no friend to me. She's a traitor! And in case you haven't noticed, Javeer's our leader and this is the Colony of Javeer, not Boro anymore."

"You're the traitor, not Bronya! Javeer's no leader. He doesn't care about you or your family. He's not going to make Boro a better place for us to live. He's a tyrant who's sacrificing the lives of Boro's citizens so he can get rich. And in case you hadn't noticed, he's slowly killing us all, one by one—or can't you see beyond one month's supply of food?"

"Gorbun knows where Matt's laptop is," said Nadia. "I got that much out of him. He says his friend still has it."

"This true?" asked Keir.

Gorbun didn't answer.

Keir threw Gorbun to the ground, pinned him with his knee and held his fist above Gorbun's face.

"I said, is this true?" said Keir, stressing every word.

Gorbun flashed him a defiant look.

"I swear I'll beat you into the ground if you don't answer me right now!" said Keir, shaking with anger.

"Keir, please . . . please stop!" begged Nadia.

Keir refused to give in to his sister's pleas. His head pounded with the stress, but now was not the time to relent.

"Keir!" Nadia cried. "Don't!"

But Keir was determined. He pulled his arm back, ready to strike.

"Okay! Okay! Enough!" said Gorbun quickly. "Okay, it's true. My friend has the black box. Now get off me!"

Keir took a deep breath, stood up and allowed the boy to get to his feet.

Gorbun staggered back against the wall and brushed his hair away from his eyes. "My friend wouldn't give it to me unless I gave him six bundles of wood," he said, panting heavily. "So I told the Gulden Guards that I was fighting with your sister on the pier and it got thrown into the sea."

"And they arrested her without any other proof?" Keir said, hardly believing the injustice of it all.

"They said my word was good enough and that they needed every member of the Underground off the streets."

"I'll bet the Gulden Guards offered to pay you again if you provided more names," said Keir.

Gorbun shrugged. "What if they did?"

"Don't you believe in telling the truth?" asked Keir. "Why don't I go to the Gulden Guards and make up some story about you? Then let's see if you get carted off to the mine."

Gorbun's defiant expression melted and a look of fear crossed his face. "You wouldn't, would you?"

"Sure. Why not?" said Keir, throwing his arms in the air and then shoving Gorbun one more time. "You've betrayed me and my family. My sister's been taken away. What more have I got to lose? Let's see . . . why don't I trade you for my sister? I'm sure I can think of some useful information to give Horando Javeer that would be worth her life for yours."

Gorbun gasped. "You wouldn't!"

Keir looked him in the eyes. "No, you're right, I wouldn't. Why? Because I *have* got something more to lose—my honor and self-respect." He pressed his face into Gorbun's. "I'm honest and loyal," he seethed. "People know they can trust me. That's what I've got . . . and that's what I'll always have. What have you got? One month's supply of food. Who do you think will trust you after this?

Who will help your family when you're sick and can't get food? No one helps a traitor."

"But I didn't turn my friend in when he wouldn't give me the computer," said Gorbun.

Nadia stood with gaping mouth, staring at him. "I should think not!"

"Then maybe there's some dignity in you after all," said Keir. "Are you ready to make right your wrong?"

"How?" Gorbun's voice trembled. "I can't get your sister back and I can't say I lied because they'll arrest me too."

"Get the computer from your friend at whatever cost and bring it to me. It may not save my sister but it will help someone else I know—and it may just help us all. This time you'll do it right or I'll see to it that you and your family are outcasts in this city. If you betray me, I guarantee that not one person will speak to you or help you for as long as you live."

Gorbun nodded. "Okay, okay. I'll get the computer."

"What about Bronya?" asked Nadia.

Keir swallowed hard. Bronya's situation was desperate, but he didn't want Nadia to know that. "Bronya's strong and I have faith. I'll pray hard that someone will help me find a way to get her out of Central Jail." He turned to Gorbun and thrust him in the direction of Wharf Street. "Now go and get the computer! I've got wood to collect for the night, and then I'll be waiting for you in the Fisherman's Market."

Gorbun frowned. "Why there?"

"No questions. Just be there," said Keir. "You've got one hour—and only one hour."

* * * * *

"So it's *two* players this time," muttered Targon. That was different. He watched Jake accept the first challenge of Level 4 and use something he called a joystick to navigate a teenage boy with dark wild hair down a snowy street.

"Seen this place before?" asked Jake.

Targon stared at the screen and shook his head. "It's not anywhere I've ever been."

Jake turned quickly to look at him and sneered. "Duh. . . dork," he said. "I meant have you seen this place in another level of this computer game?"

Targon quickly tried to recover. "Well, duh . . ." he mimicked. "*I* meant that it's not anywhere I've been in another level."

Jake grunted and continued navigating the teenager down the street.

Targon focused on the game, relieved he'd recovered from his embarrassing mistake. "It's the same place we saw earlier—just in the day instead of at night, and there's a foot of snow on the ground. See that boarded building? It's the same."

"Yeah, I knew that," said Jake, but his tone was unconvincing. "There you go, it says 'The Dark End of Javeer' at the bottom of the screen."

"So what do we have to do?"

"In order for us to meet up with the Underground we have to collect at least fifty points."

"How do we do that?" asked Targon.

Jake scanned the instructions. "We've got to take this kid . . . it says his name is Keir . . . down this street . . . Wharf Street . . . to collect certain supplies he needs."

"What kind of supplies?"

"In games like this it's usually fuel, food and weapons. Hey, didn't you do this in the other levels?"

"Umm . . . yeah, I guess. Lingoones and heat shields in Level 1, nourishment and tranquilizer guns in Level 2," said Targon, remembering the thick pink liquid he had drunk in Karn. "And in Level 3 it was Bee's great vegetable stew and capriclan crabs."

"Capri-what?"

Targon laughed. "So what's it going to be this time?"

Jake stopped the Keir character outside an entrance to a building that looked almost completely in ruins. "Let's go in here and see what we can find."

"Okay."

"Easy does it," said Jake, taking Keir to the right of the door. "It's pretty dark in here. Don't know what dangers are lurking. I'll take him up two flights. This door or that one?"

"Uh . . . the far one," said Targon, not knowing why he made that choice.

"See anything?" asked Jake.

"Go right a bit. There . . . in the corner. It's an old

table, and some broken chairs. Could that be what we want?" Suddenly a fanfare of trumpets sounded, and a white box flashed up on the screen. "What's it say?" asked Targon.

"It says 'fuel ten points each piece'. We'll collect three of those fat table legs—that's thirty points—and that's all we're allowed," said Jake, navigating Keir back down the stairs and out onto the snow-covered street.

Another trumpet fanfare was followed by another white box in the corner of the screen. "Now what?" asked Targon.

"It says to bank the fuel and find food."

"Go for it," said Targon.

Jake furrowed his brow and pulled up the bank option on the screen. "Okay, done. Where next?"

"How about over there? The sign says . . ." Targon paused to sound it out. "Fisherman's Market Hall."

"Good reading. That's got to be our food. What do you reckon it'll be?"

Targon frowned, unsure whether Jake was acting dumb or trying to crack a joke. "Duh . . . fish," he replied, mimicking Jake's gruff tone.

Jake snorted.

Targon watched as Jake carefully navigated Keir up the steps of the elegant building and through the carved doors. Keir's footsteps echoed through the computer speakers as Jake walked him across the wooden floor of the empty room.

"Don't see food or fuel here," said Jake. "We'll try

somewhere else."

Targon shook his head. "No, let's stay. Fisherman's Market's got to be the clue. Try that door at the back of the room."

Jake maneuvered Keir to open the door. "Great—more stairs. Down this time. There must be a basement."

"The rhyme said to find the Underground. That could have a double meaning . . . to find the organization, *the Underground,* or to find *the underground* of a building. There could be a storeroom at the bottom." Targon was frustrated.

"Anything's worth trying once," said Jake. "Okay, you were right—there's another door. But for some reason Keir won't go in. That means we've made a wrong move."

"Great. This'll take forever," Targon groaned just as another box flashed on the screen. "What's it say this time?"

"Collect food reward before entering."

Targon sighed. "We'll have to go back up and look around some more."

Jake marched Keir up the stairs into the center of the hall and began turning him around through a full 360 degrees.

"We've seen that cupboard at least twice now," said Targon. "Open it. It's the only possible place."

"Okay, but if it's empty we'll do what I said and try another building."

"Agreed."

Keir opened the cupboard doors and there on the shelves were five loaves of bread, three sacks of potatoes and at least ten large swordfish.

"Ten points each item," said Jake. "One loaf, one sack of potatoes and one fish—that's another thirty points, which gives us sixty total. More than enough."

"Great! Let's take them and go," said Targon, excited that at last they were getting somewhere.

Jake stopped.

"What's the problem?" snapped Targon.

"Keep your pants on!" retorted Jake. "We've got to place our food collection in the supplies bank and register our points before we can play on."

"Oh, right, sure," said Targon, trying to curtail his eagerness. They had to do this right if he wanted to win the level and meet up with Matt and Varl again. Thank goodness Jake knew how these games worked.

"Done. Okay, let's go back down the stairs," said Jake.

Targon caught his breath as Keir reached the bottom. This time a boy with long hair stood in front of the door. Targon could hardly believe it. "What's that in his hand?" he asked Jake, although he already knew the answer.

"Some sort of black box," said Jake. "Hang on, there are more instructions on the screen. It says 'You have completed your first challenge. Now take the reward from Gorbun and meet the Underground.'"

"Do it. Let Keir take it."

"Okay! Give me time," snapped Jake.

"It looks like a laptop computer to me," said Targon,

watching Keir turn it over in his hands. He gulped. Across the lid of the computer was a deep crack that he'd seen many times. It was Matt's laptop. He smiled to himself and felt suddenly reassured. But that information would have to stay in his thoughts. It was not something he could share with Jake.

"So, ready to go through the door?" asked Jake.

"Sure," said Targon, his heart racing. Matt's computer was all the confirmation he needed that he and Jake were doing something right. But where were Matt and Varl? Would he have to play the entire level without them—and only watch from the outside?

This time Jake managed to open the door and moved Keir inside with ease.

Targon gasped. Sitting on a chair in front of a blazing fire was a boy so much like Matt that Targon could not draw his eyes away from the screen. But the boy's hands and feet were tied!

At least he'd found Matt—but this was not what he had expected to see.

* * * * *

Matt heard the door open. He turned his eyes from the leaping flames to see Keir enter the room.

Lorcan shot to his feet and walked forward to block Keir's path. "Stop right there. You're not going near him."

"Come on, Lorcan, I just wanted to show him this." Keir moved closer to Matt and held out a black box.

Matt's heart skipped a beat. Yes, it was definitely his laptop. He could see the familiar crack on the lid. "You've found it! Where was it?"

"It was buried in the snow on the steps of the old bank. Some boy found it and was arguing with his friend over who should have it when Bronya saw them."

"Good for her."

"I'll take that!" said Lorcan, snatching it out of Keir's hands.

"Careful!" shouted Matt, instinctively reaching to grab it and then finding that his wrists were tied. He growled in frustration. "My computer contains vital information. You drop that and I swear you'll destroy *any* chance you had of getting rid of Horando Javeer."

Lorcan took a firmer hold of the laptop. "We'll see," he said, turning and sitting down again. "Sorcha and Fionn will be back any minute and you can plead your case to them."

Keir walked over to him. "My sister has just been arrested for her part in finding this device. That's how valuable it is, Lorcan!"

"She's been what?" asked Matt.

"The kid who found your computer handed Bronya over to the Gulden Guards claiming that she's part of the Underground."

"Why would he do that?"

"He got a big reward from the Gulden Guards—food and fuel, of course."

"I'm really sorry, Keir," said Matt. "I'll help you get her back—just as soon as your friends let me go, I promise."

Keir turned to Lorcan. "Please untie Matt. He's not

going anywhere. Can't you see that he's here to help?"

Lorcan shook his head. "Sorry. It'll take a unanimous decision from the Dark End Underground Council."

"Well then, I hope that your vote counts equally," said Matt. He had a feeling that Sorcha made the decisions and Lorcan and Fionn just went along with them.

Lorcan frowned at him. "I don't like what you are implying by that comment." He turned to Keir and said, "You realize that Sorcha will be furious when she hears about your sister. Your family is now under suspicion and so the Gulden Guards will watch you carefully."

"What exactly do you mean?" said Keir.

"I'm warning you that the Underground may no longer want you working as a runner. If it were up to me, I'd get rid of you right now. You're a security risk."

"Who's a security risk?" asked Sorcha as she entered the room, Fionn hot on her heels like a dog running after his master.

Keir sighed heavily.

"Well, Lorcan?" demanded Sorcha.

"Bronya Logan has been arrested. Some kid turned her in to the Gulden Guards claiming that she's a member of the Underground."

Sorcha's annoyance was obvious as she folded her arms across her chest. "Well then, Keir, I'm afraid I have to agree with Lorcan. We can't take a chance that you're also a target. Every minute that you're here, you're a security risk. We've worked for nearly twenty years to build up this organization—I will not let you destroy it all in a matter of days. The success of our organization lies in small cells cleverly linked together so that few people know each other. That way if one cell is arrested, the organization can still carry on."

"You've been doing this for twenty years?" said Matt. "That's a *long* time. Be honest. What have you achieved in those twenty years? Horando Javeer is still in power, and he's steadily killing off the people of Boro. At the rate you're going there'll be no one left to fight for."

Sorcha's face reddened in fury. "How dare you speak to me that way! Such rudeness! You impertinent young man, you know nothing of what we have accomplished."

"I'm just telling you exactly what I see," said Matt. "Javeer is still here!"

"Planning takes time. It has to be done carefully and thoroughly, allowing for any eventuality," Sorcha said indignantly.

"True. But while you have spent years planning, the people of Boro have been terrified and hungry, and thousands have been killed in the mines. Don't you see? You don't have years! I can help you overthrow Javeer quickly. Bronya Logan found out who had my laptop. And now I have it back."

"Enough! Bronya Logan has been arrested because she found your computer! Do you not realize that Horando Javeer will soon know of your presence here in Boro and of your laptop computer?"

"In fact, he may already know," mumbled Lorcan.

Sorcha shook her head. "It's a real shame because I

have just had it confirmed that you, Matt Hammond, have indeed come from Gova and might have been very useful to us. But now you and Keir are nothing but security risks. Because of you, our council must now change its meeting place."

"You haven't heard anything Matt has said, have you?" said Keir.

Sorcha ignored his comment. "Lorcan, untie him. Matt, you are free to go, but I don't want to see you, Keir or your computer anywhere near any member of the Dark End Underground Council again."

Matt rubbed his wrists and wiggled his free fingers. "No problem. We're going."

Keir sighed. "Big mistake, Sorcha. Can't you see that our small Underground network has done nothing against Javeer and his men? You need Matt Hammond." He turned to Lorcan and Fionn. "Some council. It seems to me that the decisions are made by one person."

"We agree," said Lorcan and Fionn in unison.

"Agree all you like," said Matt. He took his computer from Lorcan and held it above his head. "You've no idea what information this computer holds. I doubt if you remember what a computer is after nearly twenty years. Just you wait and see."

"Information! Huh!" grunted Sorcha. "Information will not rid us of Horando Javeer! I just hope you don't get killed because of your arrogance."

Chapter 6

"I'll take this one," said Varl, sitting on the bottom of a metal-framed bunk bed right by the bathroom door. "It'll be convenient."

With a huge running jump Sarven hauled himself up onto the top bunk. "Then I guess this'll have to be mine."

Varl turned away from Sarven to look at his new surroundings. When they'd disembarked from the truck Varl had eagerly rushed inside to escape the cold wind. But in that short space of time he'd figured out that each building was a self-contained housing unit resting on wooden supports about two feet off the ground.

He was surprised as he looked around. The building was actually much larger than it had seemed from the outside. It was sparse but clean and had a door at each end. One door led onto the street and the other into a communal bathroom. Twenty sets of bunks ten feet apart were positioned on one side of the room. Against the opposite wall, under narrow rectangular windows, were square wooden tables with four chairs around each. Varl counted them: ten windows and ten tables with seating for forty.

The floor was roughly constructed of thick wooden planks nailed down. There were no curtains and only two lights were suspended from ceiling beams at each end of the room. He wiggled his toes in the gentle stream of warm air rising from a vent in the floor.

"Heat," said Varl. "At least we'll be warm."

The starkness reminded him of his home in Zaul. He shuddered. He had been a prisoner there and he was a prisoner here. This place was not meant to be comfortable. It would be a place to sleep and eat—nothing more.

There were forty beds in the room. Twenty-three men and four women had left Central Jail with him that morning. Undoubtedly another group of prisoners would soon arrive and fill the remaining twelve beds.

Many prisoners were huddled together talking. From the serious tone in their voices and the grim look on their faces, Varl knew that they were as apprehensive as he was. He wondered how many of them would ever leave this place alive.

"So what do you think happens next?" asked Varl, trying to dismiss the gruesome thoughts about their fate.

Sarven jumped down from the top bunk and turned toward the opening door. "I think we're about to find out, old man."

The room instantly became silent. Varl braced himself as at least a dozen armed Gulden Guards marched in. He'd already learned to fear the sound of heavy boots and golden chains clinking together.

"Prisoners, stand by your beds," came an order.

Varl moved quickly to the end of his bunk, eyeing the

guards with suspicion. There was little difference between their muscular builds. All had rugged weather-beaten faces and long matted hair that was roughly tied back. He wondered if Horando Javeer had selected them for their similar appearance. The only one who stood out was the guard who had issued the order. He was at least six inches taller than the others and had a handlebar mustache that was curled slightly at the ends. He wore a large gold hoop pierced through one nostril and even larger hoops in each ear. His long hair was noticeably stuffed into a black cap with the letters HJG embroidered on the front. As Varl was eyeing him, the guard spoke again.

"I am Captain Culmore and I'm the duty officer in charge of your shift. You will listen carefully to your assignments." He looked down at a clipboard in his right hand.

"Assignments?" whispered Sarven.

"Who spoke?" demanded Culmore in a controlled voice without looking up from his board.

No one answered. Culmore's calm business-like expression suddenly changed. His eyes narrowed and he glowered. "I asked who spoke," he spat. "Answer me, or there'll be no food tonight for anyone in this bunkhouse."

"I did," said Varl quickly.

Sarven shot him a horrified glance.

Culmore handed his board to another guard in exchange for a whip and walked slowly and precisely to the end of the line. He stared down into Varl's eyes. "I hope you're not going to be a problem."

Varl looked at the whip coiled in Culmore's right hand. He swallowed hard and answered, "Not at all, sir. I asked the boy what you said. I'm getting old and can't hear too well."

"Well, you'll have to listen harder," grunted Culmore. He shoved Varl backwards against the bunk and smacked the whip hard on the floor close to his feet, cutting the thin fabric of Varl's pants.

Varl winced. Sarven shot him another glance, gratitude visible in his eyes.

Culmore picked up his clipboard and continued pacing. "As I was saying before I was rudely interrupted, you will now get your assignments. This is bunkhouse 157. Do not forget the number. You will be punished severely if you are found in any other bunkhouse. You may not leave the bunkhouse unless instructed to do so by one of the guards. Your work assignment in the mine will start at dawn tomorrow. This bunkhouse will work shift B, which begins at 7:00 a.m. and ends at 3:00 p.m. You will be taken to mine shaft 1 by your mine guide tomorrow morning and you will be given further instructions when you get there. Is that clear?"

Everyone mumbled in agreement.

Culmore tucked his clipboard under his arm and announced, "Food will be delivered within the hour." With that he marched out, followed by the other guards.

As soon as the door closed, Sarven turned to Varl. "Thanks, old man. I owe you one."

"No problem."

"Are you okay?"

Varl nodded. "I'm fine, thanks. The whip only cut through my clothes. Culmore probably went easier on me because of my age than he would have on you. Besides, you're already a good friend. You've been a comfort to me."

"The feeling's mutual," said Sarven. "But, we do have a deal, remember?"

"Ah, yes, we do indeed. I'd almost forgotten. I'm your protection from the Gnashers," said Varl. He gnashed his teeth menacingly and then broke into a broad grin.

Varl waited for a laugh, but Sarven shook his head, sat down on Varl's bed and buried his head in his hands.

"You're really worried about these Gnasher creatures, aren't you?" said Varl.

"Uh-huh. And they're not creatures, they're mine monsters."

"So it's not just some story you made up earlier to get my sympathy?"

"Hardly," said Sarven, looking up with big doleful eyes. "How could I invent something like Gnashers?"

"Hmmm," said Varl, wondering if the young man had ever heard of imagination. "But you've never seen one of these Gnasher things, right?"

Sarven shook his head. "I've just seen what they do to humans. They leave millions of little teeth marks all over the bodies. Ugh! What a gross death!" He shuddered and drew in a deep breath. "The Gulden Guards are terrified of them. They won't go down the mine shafts anymore because so many guards have been killed."

"So they're sending the citizens of Boro down the mine instead."

Sarven nodded. "You've got the picture."

Varl sighed and sat next to him. "We'll get through this, I promise you. Somehow we'll get out of here alive."

Sarven rolled his eyes. "Yeah, right. Like that's going to happen with all these guards here."

"Tomorrow we'll start planning. We'll observe guard movements and we'll make it our business to find out everything we can about all the equipment within the electric fences around the mine."

"Electric?" questioned Sarven. "But we don't have electricity in Boro."

"Sure you do. Didn't you see the three fences as we drove through the main gates, and all of the huge cables overhead? See the lights in here? Now look down at the floor—the hot air is being pumped through the ducts. All electric."

"But we've not had electricity in Boro since before I was born. When Horando Javeer arrived, he diverted most of the water from the reservoirs and the electricity from the power stations to run his gold mine. Everyone had to cut down trees for firewood. Now it's got so bad there are hardly any trees left and people are chopping up and burning furniture, or anything else they can get their hands on."

"Did you have gas and oil back then?"

"Yes, but we were already short before Javeer arrived. I hadn't seen a truck until today—only heard about them from older people. Everyone has to walk these days."

"This is a true tale of horror," said Varl. "Javeer devastated the land and ruined the economy, not to mention your lives. And all for what?"

Sarven shrugged. "Gold, of course. Javeer is one greedy man."

"Not for much longer," said Varl determinedly. "I'll come up with some way to get us out of here and then we'll find a way to destroy the mine."

Sarven shook his head. "Yeah, right. Good luck, old man. You're taking on the impossible, if you ask me."

Chapter 7

Targon gulped. He stared at the boy on the screen. There was no doubt about it; that was Matt sitting on the chair in front of the blazing fire. How strange it felt to be on the outside looking in. It didn't seem that Jake had noticed the resemblance, and Targon guessed that he wouldn't make any connection. After all, who in their right mind would ever imagine his kid brother inside a computer game?

"Yes!" Jake said with gusto. "We completed the task." He turned up the volume on the speakers.

Targon listened to the conversation between Matt, Keir and several adults who had entered the room. They spoke in stilted, computerized voices. "They're definitely part of the Underground," said Targon, wishing he could be there with Matt.

"Did you hear what they just said? Those people from the Underground aren't going to help the boy in the chair," said Jake, looking glum. As he peered at the screen a look of surprise crossed his face. "It says his name is Matt." He grunted. "Weird that he has the same name as my brother. He even *looks* like my brother. Awww! How naf! Matt probably set up his name as a player and selected a character that looked like him. I'll bet you anything that he's our second player."

"Well, the rhyme did say two players. Remember it also said that the Underground wouldn't be easy to persuade and that they'd see us as a threat to their network."

"Looks like that's come true—but I figured we'd get *some* help," Jake complained.

"We did," said Targon. "We've got Keir on our side. He's part of the Underground."

Jake turned to look at him. "Well, if that's all the help we're gonna get, we're in serious trouble."

"It's better than nothing," replied Targon, trying to keep optimistic. "We've got to locate the Keeper before we go any further and work out how to destroy him."

Jake scrolled down the menu bar. "We need weapons then."

"Not until we know who the enemy is. You can't choose your weapon before you know what you have to destroy."

"It's gotta be that guy Horando who invaded."

Targon shook his head. "There's been a catch in every other level. It's never been who we thought it was."

Jake grunted. "Okay, smart guy. What do you suggest?"

"Click on *'Keeper'* and see what it says."

Jake groaned when he saw another rhyme. "Not another one of these dumb things to solve."

"It wasn't hard last time. What does it say?"

"Two Keepers. We have to find two Keepers, not one."

"Are you sure?"

"'Course I am. It says plain as day, 'two Keepers.'"

Targon scratched his head. "Two players and now two Keepers. This is really different."

"We're on expert difficulty. Things always get tough."

"Oh," said Targon. "So how do you suggest we find the two Keepers?"

Jake shrugged. "The rhyme says we have to travel deep underground."

"That could mean mines or caves or something," said Targon.

"Duh," said Jake in his usual 'anyone knows that' tone.

"We need a map," said Targon, ignoring Jake's last insult.

Jake pointed to the screen. "'Map' is Number 1 on the menu bar. I'll pull it up. If there are mines or caves marked then we'll know where to go next."

Targon sighed. He couldn't understand Matt's fascination with computer games. This seemed so slow and boring compared to the exciting adventures he'd had. He couldn't believe that he was actually wishing he were there—back inside the game with Matt. "Go ahead. See what you can find out," he said, slumping back in his chair.

"Yes!" hissed Jake, punching the air with his fist. "Told you so. There's a gold mine in the East End of Boro. I knew it. We'll be going down a mine next."

"But we still don't know who the two Keepers are," Targon groaned. "Does it give us any clues as to who they might be?"

"Give us a minute!" snapped Jake. "Man, you're impatient! I bet our next task will be to collect weapons. I don't care what you say. We've gotta get weapons so we're prepared for anything the enemy throws at us."

Targon drew in a deep breath. He felt as though he was going nowhere fast. *Please put me back in the game,* he thought. *Anything's better than this.* Jake was a pain. He talked as if he were drawing up battle plans, yet they still didn't have an enemy. How would he know what weapons to collect if he didn't know what kind of battle they would be fighting? Targon had to do something before Jake got them into a whole heap of trouble. At this rate they'd lose the game without even trying—and then what would happen to Matt?

* * * * *

Bronya had been in Central Jail for only a few minutes when four of the Gulden Guards appeared and unlocked her cell. They dragged her roughly into the street. She was frozen in her thin sweater and torn skirt. She imagined that she was wearing her old woolen coat and for a fleeting moment she felt warmer. As they passed by the rows of houses, she saw faces appear at the windows and heard whispering in the alleyways. She wondered if Keir and Matt were watching as the guards marched her up the hill toward the ancient castle that was once the Boro parliament building.

Why were the Gulden Guards taking her to the castle?

Was her punishment to work in the kitchens or as a servant or cleaner? Anything would be better than rotting in Central Jail.

The lights that twinkled in the windows of the narrow castle towers seemed foreboding, almost as if they were warning her to stay away. The old drawbridge lowered, hitting the ground with a bang. Bronya watched the portcullis slowly rise, and winced as the metal rattled and screeched. She shivered as the guards marched her under its huge metal spikes.

A wave of dread passed over her. Would she be thrown into the castle dungeons? She bit her lip as they crossed the cobbled courtyard toward the eastern tower where the dungeons were located. Is that where she was headed? Maybe Central Jail would have been preferable after all.

One of the guards suddenly grabbed her elbow and turned her toward the wide stone steps that led into the great hall. Bronya drew breath. Perhaps she had escaped the dungeons.

She gasped as she entered the great hall and gazed upon the massive sweeping timber arches that supported the high, carved ceiling. Unlike all the other buildings in Javeer this one had not been stripped of its wood. The room was furnished with elegant upholstered chairs and the walls adorned with enormous paintings depicting Boron scenery. At the far end of the room a roaring fire in the gigantic stone fireplace cast a warm glow across the shiny marble floor.

"Sit," instructed the guard.

"Here?" questioned Bronya, pointing to one of the fine velvet chairs. The guard nodded and so she lowered herself slowly into it, unable to believe that something so comfortable could exist or that she should be allowed to sit in it.

"Why am I here?" Bronya asked.

The guard said nothing.

Bronya fidgeted nervously. She looked around the room wondering what was going to happen next. The elaborately carved door next to the fireplace opened, and into the room strode a tiny man with straggly mousy hair and large pointed ears that stuck out from his head. He stood for a minute and fiddled with the wide cuffs on his shimmering green shirt as if weighing her up. His tight green leggings and thick fur-trimmed gold cape made him look like something out of a medieval story. Then he strode toward her. Bronya tried to contain a giggle as her gaze fell upon his feet. His hefty black boots made his thin little legs look ridiculous.

"Kneel," instructed the guard, pushing her off the chair and onto the floor.

Bronya knelt and lowered her head. *Who is this strange little man?* she thought.

"Get up, girl," said the small man in a high-pitched scratchy voice.

Bronya scrambled quickly to her feet and raised her head slowly, boldly meeting his beady green eyes. She altered her posture and pushed back her shoulders when she realized that she was taller than him.

A cold expression settled on his face. "I am Horando Javeer and you, Bronya Logan, are in serious trouble."

"H—H—Horando Javeer?" She choked on the name. This couldn't be Horando Javeer. Javeer was a frightening man, larger than life, strong, destructive and powerful—not tiny and scrawny with a high squeaky voice. It couldn't be him!

"Horando Javeer? Huh! Is this some kind of a joke?" asked Bronya in a contrary tone.

"Show some respect!" said the guard. He struck the right side of her head with his hand.

Bronya staggered sideways and instinctively grabbed her burning ear. The room seemed to spin, but she regained her balance quickly and faced Javeer, more determined than ever to show her courage.

"Enough," said Javeer, waving his hand at the guard. "So, Miss Bronya Logan, you find it hard to believe that I am Horando Javeer, Keeper? Don't you know that great leaders are not judged by their size and stature? I have the respect of my followers and the power of life and death over my subjects. You will do well to remember that when speaking to me."

Bronya nodded, realizing her stupidity in angering the man. "Okay," she muttered.

"You will address me as Keeper. Is that understood?"

"Yes, Keeper."

"Good. I'm glad we have that clear." He offered her a forgiving smile. "You may sit down."

Bronya felt as though her insides had been twisted into a knot and turned twice. She could hardly believe that this puny little man could wield so much power over the Gulden Guards and fill her with so much dread. And yet she would not allow him to see her fear. She watched him warily as she sat down.

"What do you want of me . . . Keeper? I haven't committed a crime or done any harm to you or your Gulden Guards."

Javeer smiled. He moved closer, standing directly in front of her. "A courageous young lady," he said, tapping his chin with his forefinger. "It's a pity that you are such a liar."

Bronya felt hot and then cold. "I am *not* a member of the Underground, contrary to what you have been told by some snitch who feeds you lies to get food and fuel."

"No, you are not a member of the Underground. That I don't dispute. But your actions may help the Underground, of which your brother *is* a member!"

Bronya frowned. "No, he isn't!" she replied as convincingly as she could.

The Keeper clapped his hands together. "Bravo! Protecting your family. That's very noble—but stupid if you want to stay alive."

"I don't know anything about my brother being part of the Underground—I swear. My ma is very sick. Keir works hard collecting food and wood for us all."

"Hmmm. Then tell me about the stranger that arrived from Gova a few days ago. Your brother has been seen with him several times. What can you tell me about the stranger's computer?"

"A stranger from Gova?" replied Bronya innocently. "And what is a computer?"

The Keeper leaned over Bronya, gripping her arm until she winced with the pain.

"I'll ask you once more. What do you know about a stranger from Gova? Why did he come to the Dark End of Javeer? Tell me and you will go free. Defy me and you'll regret it."

Bronya shook her head. "I don't know *anything* about *anyone* from Gova."

Javeer shook the chair. His eyes flashed with rage. "Protecting your brother, I can understand. Protecting a stranger who may be an enemy of the Colony of Javeer is pure folly. Do you really want to be banished to the mine, where you will almost certainly die?"

"I don't know anything about any stranger," said Bronya defiantly. "Send me down the mine, for all I care." Her heart pounded as she waited for his response. Had she been stupid to protect Matt? After all, what did she really know about him?

Javeer hesitated, as if he were measuring her up. He stood upright, his brow furrowed. Bronya's fear increased as she awaited her fate.

"So be it," he said, a chill in his voice. "You have made your decision and I have made mine. Take her *immediately* to the gold mine. You will serve a two-year sentence."

Bronya clenched her jaw to kill the sob in her throat and struggled to maintain her composure. After all, what had she expected? She had just defied Horando Javeer. *Be thankful you are still alive, Bron,* she told herself. *You'll survive the mine. You're strong enough.*

Javeer turned away from her gaze and began talking to the guard in a low voice. She strained to hear what they were saying. "Watch her carefully," he murmured. "Spread the word around the Dark End, and be ready."

She walked out holding her head high, proud that she hadn't betrayed her brother or Matt, who she knew had come to help them. But her gut was telling her that something wasn't right. She remembered Javeer's words to the guard. What had he meant by 'Spread the word around the Dark End and be ready'? Be ready for what?

Bronya felt suddenly weak as she put the pieces together. Her mood veered sharply to despair. She had played right into the tyrant's hands. Javeer hadn't wanted her to give in to his questioning. He would have thrown her in the mines no matter what she'd said.

Now the guards would spread the word that she'd been sentenced to two years, hoping to draw out the members of the Underground. Horando Javeer was looking for a way to destroy the entire Underground network, and he was using her as bait.

Chapter 8

Keir slammed the front door of his house, yanked off his hat and threw his coat over the wooden peg. "I'm so mad! I can't believe the Underground Council kicked me out!"

"Well, I can see their point," said Matt, shivering as he removed his jacket. "The Underground did what they thought was right—protecting their runners and trying to keep their organization together."

"Organization? What organization? I've spent two years running between different Underground Councils all over Boro, collecting and carrying information about Javeer and his guards. Where has it got us? There aren't any plans to get rid of him. Our situation has got worse, not better."

"They're just scared," said Matt. "They have no weapons and little food. They're weak in every way possible . . . and they know it."

"But the longer we wait the weaker we will get," Keir said as he strode down the hall.

"I agree," said Matt, following him.

"Bronya's in trouble and now, because the Underground Council won't work with us, her life is in more danger than I had thought," added Keir.

"How so?" asked Matt.

"I'll explain later," said Keir, opening the door to the back room. "I need to check on Nadia and Ma, but I don't want to discuss this in front of them."

"Okay, but it seems we have to do something quickly. I've got plans right here in my hands." He lifted the laptop.

When they opened the door, Matt saw the fire was dying. Nadia was desperately trying to stoke it back to life, tears rolling down her cheeks.

"Here, let me do that," said Keir in a soft voice. He lifted another log onto the fire and stoked it until it blazed again. "Where's Ma?"

"In bed. She's much worse since Bronya was . . ." Nadia broke down into heavy sobs. "It's like she's given up hope."

"Hey, it's okay," said Keir, hugging his sister. "Bronya's strong. We'll get her back, I promise. I'll go and talk to Ma in a little while."

A lump came into Matt's throat. He could hardly imagine what they were feeling. He had only known Bronya for a few hours, and already he missed her laughter. The freezing house seemed even colder without her. "We're putting a plan together right now," said Matt, opening his laptop and trying to spread some cheer.

"Really?" said Nadia, sniffing and wiping her eyes with the back of her hand. She sat on the mat next to him.

Matt drew in a deep breath as he booted up his computer. The screen illuminated and he was relieved to see that the battery was fully charged. At least something was going right today.

"So, how exactly do we put a plan together?" asked Keir.

"Easy. You'll see. We'll have clues in the form of rhymes to help us," said Matt, trying to sound confident.

"Clues? Rhymes?" questioned Nadia. "You make it sound like a game."

Matt smiled. How often he had heard that comment on his travels. Of course, Nadia was right—it was a game. But most of the time the adventures were so real that it didn't feel like a game at all. "Here we go. Ready to listen?"

Nadia nodded.

Matt turned up the volume and placed his laptop on the floor where they could all see. A deep voice, now so familiar to Matt, welcomed them.

Welcome back, players of Keeper of the Kingdom. You have already selected two players and entered Level 4, Keeper of the Colony. Previous game play has been saved. You may continue to navigate the Colony of Javeer on expert difficulty.

"I don't get it," said Keir. "What's *Keeper of the Kingdom*?"

"It's all just information in code from the Sons of Liberty so that I can access what I need," said Matt as convincingly as he could. "Level 4, *Keeper of the Colony,* is the key. Remember I told you that this task is considered Level 4 by the Sons of Liberty?"

Keir nodded.

Matt stopped abruptly. Wait a minute. He looked back at the screen. Had he read that right? Did it say *two* players? He hadn't agreed to that, had he? And why did it say that previous game play had been saved when he hadn't even begun this level?

Just then an enormous aircraft with rotating propellers zigzagged across the screen. The deafening roar of the engines caused Nadia to cover her ears and shrink back from the computer.

"Curfew patrol," she said with bitterness.

"That's right here. That's the Dark End!" exclaimed Keir, pointing to the tall buildings with smashed windows on the screen. "Look! There's the Fisherman's Market Hall."

"I can hear the foghorn," said Nadia. "And there's the wharf and the seawall."

Keir leaned closer to the screen. "This is impressive stuff. It's like looking at a map but in pictures. How did the Sons of Liberty get pictures of the Dark End?"

"Spies," said Matt without really thinking what Keir had asked him. Something wasn't quite right, but he wasn't sure what. Had somebody already opened his laptop and begun playing the level? "Give me a minute. I've got to look at my program history before we go any further," he muttered.

Keir got up to stoke the fire.

"Program history?" asked Nadia. "What's that?"

"What I did last," said Matt, looking back at the game records. He froze, his eyes glued to the screen. No, it couldn't be true! The first step in Level 4, *Locating the Underground*, had been completed only minutes ago! But how . . . and by whom? He glanced at Keir. This much was true—he had already met the Underground—but he hadn't opened his laptop until now. Could he have stumbled on the Underground by chance? His heart quickened as he read the first rhyme. *Your plans will be seen as a threat to destroy their network—not protect.* This was bizarre. Less than an hour ago, Sorcha had told him that she never wanted to see him or Keir near the Underground Council ever again.

"Keir, did anyone have this computer before you brought it to me?" asked Matt.

"Some boys found it in the snow. It was only after Bronya was arrested that I persuaded Gorbun to bring it to me."

Matt frowned.

"Something wrong?" asked Keir.

"It seems that someone has already accessed the information," said Matt.

"How is that possible?" asked Keir. "Gorbun wouldn't know what to do with that thing."

"True," said Matt. A wave of panic swept over him. He looked up at Keir. "Could Gorbun have taken my computer to Horando Javeer before giving it to you?"

Horror showed on Keir's face. "Are you thinking that the Gulden Guards are on to us? Geez, I hope this isn't another trap!   Has someone taken some of your information?"

"The information hasn't *gone* anywhere," said Matt. "It's still here on my computer. But it seems that someone else has read it before us. I just hope it isn't our enemy."

"Gorbun betrayed us once. He could easily have done it a second time," said Keir.

"Please don't say that," said Nadia. "I can't bear the thought of you being taken too, Keir."

Matt gulped. He looked uneasily around the room, half expecting to see Gulden Guards. The rhyme had said two players this time. But how could anyone else be playing the game? And who would know his password to access his game?

"We'll just have to be careful and trust no one," said Matt, pulling up the menu again. The next step in each level was always to locate the Keeper. He scrolled down the list to Number 9 and clicked on the word *'Keeper.'* "I'm going to read a rhyme. See what you make of it."

In Level 4 rules aren't the same
Locate two Keepers to win the game
One will prove a useful friend
Make a pact and he'll defend
Be warned; approach the second with care
Motives are evil and survivors rare
You'll travel deep underground
Where two worlds meet and answers are found.

"Two Keepers," Keir muttered.

"Does it mean anything to you?" asked Matt.

Keir and Nadia both shook their heads.

"Only one Keeper that I know of," said Nadia. "That's the Keeper of this horrible place—Horando Javeer."

Matt smiled at her. "Well, we have to find two. You can't think of any other Keepers?"

"Sorry," said Keir. "That word isn't used for anything around here but Horando Javeer."

Matt sighed. He couldn't have reached a dead end already, could he? "Let's read it again."

"Hold on—underground means something different here," said Keir. "It seems like the rhyme is saying we should *go* underground not *to* the Underground for help."

"Deep underground where two worlds meet," read Matt. "I agree with you."

"Could be the gold mine in Eastern Boro," said Nadia, as if thinking aloud. "It's really deep underground. I've heard people say that it's a different world down there."

"Gold mine?" questioned Matt. "Do you think Nadia's right?"

"I'd bet my life on it," said Keir. "That's the reason that Horando Javeer invaded Boro."

"The gold?" asked Matt.

"Pure greed," responded Keir. "Horando Javeer mined more gold than anyone would need in a lifetime in the first few weeks he was here. Gulden is an old word meaning gold. Javeer created the Gulden Guards to watch over his gold. They were once his miners and the mine security.

They soon became his army and bodyguards as well."

"Where is the mine?"

"About thirty miles east of here."

"Too far to walk," said Matt.

Keir nodded. "It would take a day or two."

There was a loud knock on the front door.

"Nadia, go and see who it is," said Keir.

Nadia sighed, but left the room without complaint.

Keir said nothing as Nadia left. Matt could tell from his hesitation that he didn't want Nadia to hear what he was about to say.

"Javeer empties Central Jail of prisoners several times a week," Keir began. "He sends most of the women and children to work in the castle. But all of the men, and the women who have committed the most serious crimes, are taken by gunship out to the mine and forced to work in horrendous conditions. Most don't survive."

"But didn't you say that my friend Varl may be in Central Jail?"

"And Bronya," said Keir, his head dropping. "If they decide that Bronya is a traitor she could be sent to the mine and not to the castle. I don't want Nadia or Ma to know, but by the end of the week my sister and your friend Varl may be on their way to the mine."

"Now I'm beginning to understand why you're so worried about her."

"She's strong, but wouldn't survive long down the mine," said Keir in a whisper. "I stupidly thought that the Underground Council would welcome you and work with us to rescue her from Central Jail before she even got to the mine. But now Bronya is in great danger, and all of the information I gathered won't be used."

"Yes, it will," said Matt. "*We* can still use everything you've learned to get her out of Central Jail. We'll just have to do it without the Underground—and do it fast."

Keir's face was glum. "But what can just two of us do against the Gulden Guards, and with so little time to prepare?"

"We'll think of something," said Matt.

The door opened and Nadia returned. "Someone's here to see you, Keir," she said, throwing a look of disgust at the young man behind her.

Keir looked up. Instantly he jumped to his feet in a defensive stance. "Gorbun. What are you doing here? Not a second betrayal, I hope."

Gorbun shook his head and looked remorseful. "No. No Gulden Guards with me this time, I promise." He raised his arms as if in surrender.

"Nadia, go and check on Ma," said Keir abruptly, obvious that he wanted her to leave.

"Why are you always trying to get rid of me?"

Keir frowned at her. "Please," he added.

Nadia hesitated but then left without further argument.

"I've brought you news about Bronya," said Gorbun. It's not good, I'm afraid. The Gulden Guards marched her up to the castle."

"But that *is* good, isn't it?" Matt interrupted. "Doesn't that mean she won't be sent to the mine?"

Gorbun shook his head. "A short time later, she was loaded into Javeer's personal gunship. There's lots of rumors around town."

"What rumors?" asked Keir.

"Everyone's saying that she defied Javeer. He wanted to know about your friend from Gova and his computer." Gorbun paused to glance at Matt. "She wouldn't tell him anything about either of you, so they sent her straight to the mine—a two-year sentence."

Keir sank down slowly in the chair by the fire and stared into the flames. "Are you telling the truth this time?"

"I swear," replied Gorbun.

"Then I guess I'm too late to help my sister. God protect her. She'll never survive two years in the mine."

"Don't give up. It's never too late," said Matt. "You said yourself that Bronya's strong. We've still got time—our task is just harder now. Let's find a way to get into the mine."

Keir laughed. "Difficult—especially without any help from the Underground. Have you any idea what we'll be up against? For starters, electric fences and hundreds of Gulden Guards with ST29s."

"Electric fences will be no problem," said Matt. He was trying to sound confident, but deep down he knew the task was much harder than he was making it out to be.

Keir laughed even louder. "How about *three* rows of electric fences with barbed wire on the top and forty-foot guard towers!"

"Tricky," said Matt, "but I can do it. I've done it before."

He eyed Gorbun suspiciously. The boy was taking in everything that was being said. Matt quickly added, "Just get me to the main gates and my computer will get us in." He tapped the lid of his laptop.

"Count me in," said Gorbun. "This I gotta see."

Keir raised his eyebrows.

"You *can* trust me," Gorbun said.

"You won't get anything for your help. We haven't any extra food or fuel supplies to give you," said Keir, his tone accusing.

"Don't want nothin'," said Gorbun. "I came to make amends."

Keir shrugged. "Okay. Thanks for the offer. But that's still only three of us against hundreds. It's not enough. We've got to get more help before we can do this."

"I've gotta go," said Gorbun. "Just let me know when you need me."

As Keir showed Gorbun the door, Matt studied the rhyme again. Everything Keir had said about the mine seemed to fit with the pattern of his *Keeper of the Kingdom* game. The gold mine was the reason why Javeer had invaded Boro and a rescue mission was needed. He knew he was on the right track. The game clues were telling him that.

He closed the lid of his laptop. This level of his game was set at expert difficulty and would take a lot of thought and ingenuity. Where was Targon with his bright ideas when he needed him?

Keir came back into the room. "Well, what do you

know?" he said, shaking his head. "I didn't expect Gorbun to show his face around here again."

"Do you trust him?" asked Matt.

Keir shrugged. "It's going to be hard after what he did to Bronya. But I guess everyone deserves a second chance. We'll see."

"By the way, you didn't really think I could get you through the main gates of Javeer's gold mine, did you?"

Keir laughed. "Don't worry—I knew what you were doing with Gorbun in the room. Just in case he's still working for Javeer, we definitely want him thrown off the track."

"Let's be careful," said Matt. "A lot is at stake here. I'd rather not get too many people involved."

"Agreed. But I know someone who could really help us. His name is Varak . . . Varak Morsova."

"Who's he?"

"Another runner—which is why I didn't mention him while Gorbun was here. We're not supposed to know each other."

"Yeah, I remember Sorcha saying that the Underground tries to keep its runners secret for the security of the network."

"He saved me from curfew patrol one night last winter," Keir continued. "We've been friends ever since. Varak does the run from here to the East End Underground—near the mine. I've traded information with him loads of times and I'd trust him with my life."

"Good enough for me," said Matt.

"He'll know a lot about the mine, and he's got an extra reason to see Javeer defeated. Javeer's sent three of his brothers to the mine already. Two have died, one is still there."

"That's awful! Poor Varak," said Matt. "I've got a brother, Jake. I always thought he was a real pain, but right now I sure miss him."

Keir smiled. "I know what you mean. I'd give anything to see Bron walk through that door."

"So what are we waiting for? Take me to meet Varak. We're wasting time sitting here."

"Time is precious," said Keir. "But so is food and sleep. If we're hungry and tired we won't be good for anything in this weather. We'll head out at first light."

Chapter 9

Varl sat up in his bunk when he heard a truck engine idling in the street outside.

"New prisoners arriving," said Sarven.

"Didn't take them long to find another twelve poor souls to fill these beds," said Varl, feeling disgust at Javeer's wanton disregard for human life.

He watched the door open. To his surprise only one young girl slowly shuffled in. She had dark hypnotic eyes and delicate features, and even though her short hair was roughly cut, its shiny luster added to her beauty. She stood at the door looking bewildered.

Sarven jumped down from the top bunk and hurried to greet her. No one else seemed interested in the new arrival. Varl watched the others turn back to their conversations.

"You okay, miss?" Sarven asked.

She nodded and looked around the room without saying anything.

"There's a couple of spare beds down by us," said Sarven, pointing at Varl. "They're comfortable enough. I'm Sarven Morsova, by the way. What's your name?"

"Bronya Logan," she replied, following him down the bunkhouse. "At least it's warm in here."

"It's okay, I guess. We got here this afternoon," he said, reaching his bunk. "This is my friend, Varl."

"Nice to meet you, Bronya," said Varl, wondering what she could have done to end up here.

"Did you say Varl?" questioned Bronya, her face brightening instantly. "I've heard that name before!"

Varl eased himself off the lower bunk and shook her hand. "You have? Where?"

"Someone called Matt is looking for you."

A wave of excitement passed over Varl. "Matt, my boy," he said with glee. "I knew he couldn't be far away. Is Targon with him?"

Bronya shook her head. "No, Matt's looking for Targon too. No one has seen him."

Varl felt a little deflated at that news. He ducked his head and sat back down on his bunk. "Well, if Matt's here and I'm here, Targon will be somewhere close by, I'm sure. Where is Matt? Not in Central Jail, I hope."

Bronya sat next to him. "No. He's avoided capture by Javeer so far. Matt is working with my brother Keir, who's a runner for the Dark End Underground."

"Ah! The Underground! Good, he's found them already," said Varl. Matt had quickly found the Liberators in Zaul, the Freedom Fighters in Karn and the Resistance in Gova. This was great news. It meant that Matt was already on track with Level 4 of his *Keeper of the Kingdom* game. "He didn't waste any time connecting with the Underground, did he?"

"Actually, I think it happened by chance," said Bronya.

"My brother saved him from curfew patrol and then took him to meet the Dark End Underground Council."

"I wish he'd been there to save me too! I might not have ended up here," said Varl.

"I'm sorry you had the misfortune to run into the Gulden Guards," said Bronya.

Varl smiled and took hold of Bronya's hand. He squeezed it tightly. "If anyone can get us out of here, Matt can," he said in a reassuring tone. "His little black computer is an amazing thing."

"So I'm told," said Bronya. She lowered her gaze and took a deep breath. "There's a problem there, I'm afraid."

Varl frowned. "Don't tell me he's lost it again."

"It's complicated. Before I got arrested I found out who had it but I wasn't able to get it back. I was arrested for being part of the Underground because my contact betrayed me and told Horando Javeer about the computer."

"Oh," said Varl. He looked into Bronya's huge doleful eyes and added as optimistically as he could, "Is that all? Don't worry, my girl. If I know Matt, he'll have it back by now and he'll already have a plan to get us out of here."

"That'd better include me," said Sarven, who had been listening intently to their conversation. "We had a deal, right, old man?"

"You don't think I'd leave you behind, do you?" said Varl, lowering his voice to a whisper. "You've got me this far. If I get out of here, you'll both be with me."

"Well, your friends had better not be long about it.

Tomorrow morning we're going down the mine," said Sarven. "There's no telling how long we'll survive."

"I've heard all kinds of horror stories," said Bronya. "Can't say I'm looking forward to it."

"Gnashers?" asked Varl with a grin.

Bronya shot him a piercing painful look. "You've already heard, then. If the heat and work conditions don't kill us, the Gnashers will."

Varl studied her serious expression. "You believe Gnashers exist as well?"

"Of course they exist!" Bronya shot back. "We've *all* seen the proof!"

"So why has no one ever seen a Gnasher?" asked Varl. "And do you have proof that Gnashers actually made those teeth marks?"

"You'll have loads of proof soon enough," said Bronya as the lights went out.

"Shame. Bed time," said Sarven. "I guess we get no choice in the matter. Better get under the covers in case the guards come in to check." He hauled himself onto the top bunk.

Varl yawned and felt for his blanket in the dark. He lifted his weary legs off the floor and tried to make himself comfortable on the hard mattress. It had been a day of many highs and lows, but at least he knew that Matt was here in the Colony of Javeer. But could Matt win this level of his game without him or Targon? He felt helpless stuck here in this gold mine. Or was it possible that he was already helping Matt with Level 4 of his computer game?

"Locate and destroy the Keeper and free the people," muttered Varl. Weren't those the rules of the game? What if Matt's task this time was to free the people of Boro from the clutches of Horando Javeer?

Varl suddenly wasn't dreading tomorrow. He now looked at daybreak as an opportunity. Excitement rushed through his old bones. He would begin his reconnaissance of Horando Gold Mine and learn as much as he could about the equipment . . . and the Gnashers.

*****

Targon stared at the map of Boro on the computer screen. "Boro Gold Mine," he said, sounding out each word carefully. A large black X had been drawn through the word Boro, and in its place the word Horando printed in capital letters.

"*Horando* Gold Mine," corrected Jake.

"That has to be our next task. The gold mine is the key to finding two keepers, I'll bet you anything."

Jake yawned. "So how do we get Keir to take Matt there?"

"Is there anything on the menu that might help us?" asked Targon.

"It says Number 2, '*Transportation*' right here," said Jake, clicking on the icon of a truck. A small box opened in the top corner of the screen, the map still visible beneath.

"What does it say we can use?"

Jake groaned. "It's not good. It says there are only two trucks still working. Horando Javeer destroyed the rest when he took over Boro and renamed it the Colony of Javeer. The two that remain are used to transport the Gulden Guards and prisoners going to the mine."

"So how do we get Matt and Keir to the mine?"

"Beats me," shrugged Jake. "There are three symbols, so I guess that means we have three choices: the two trucks used by the Gulden Guards, helicopter gunships used by the Gulden Guards, or a . . ." he paused and frowned. "A canoe? What's the use in that?"

Targon traced the winding river on the map with his index finger. The Boro-Boro River began in the mountains close to the Horando Gold Mine and flowed into the sea in the Dark End of Javeer. He couldn't help but smile. He couldn't read too well, but he certainly understood maps.

"Click on the river! Click on the river!" he shouted, unable to control his excitement.

"Okay! Give us time!" Jake snapped.

The swirling waters and jagged rocks of the Boro-Boro River suddenly dominated the screen. Targon shivered. Just looking at the icy banks and falling snow made him feel cold. But when he heard the howling wind he felt doubly glad he wasn't there.

"So you think we should send Matt and Keir on a canoe trip?" asked Jake.

Targon frowned. "It seemed like a good idea until I saw the Boro-Boro River." He pointed to the screen. "Just look at that fast current, the rocks everywhere and the floating tree trunks. We'd be sending them to a certain death, don't you think?"

"Depends," grunted Jake.

"On what?"

"If you trust me."

"If I trust you? What's trust got to do with anything?" asked Targon. "The river's a nightmare no matter how you look at it!"

"Yeah, but Keir and Matt don't have to get themselves down the river—*we've* got to get them down the river. Trust me! I'm great at navigating hazards in computer games. I'll have them down this baby in no time!"

"But . . ."

Jake grabbed the joystick and clicked on '*Play*' before Targon could utter any objection. Matt was about to go for the ride of his life, and Targon could only sit back, watch and pray.

Chapter 10

Matt grabbed onto the icy bank, trying to prevent himself from sliding into the fast flowing Boro-Boro River. It was hard to maintain his balance with the weight of his computer and supplies in the pack on his back. They had been walking along the banks for hours, trying to stay hidden from any Gulden Guards that might pass on the road above, and he guessed that they were still a long way from their destination. His hands were numb from digging his fingers into the snow for support. Keir was twenty yards ahead and Matt felt annoyed that he couldn't keep up.

Matt stared at the rushing water less than ten feet below him. The river was high with the melting snow. Huge tree branches bobbed up and down in the current, hitting the bank and spinning back into mid-stream as if they were weightless. His heart quickened when he realized that one mistake could send him tumbling down the bank and into the freezing water. Within seconds he'd be swept away.

"Come on, Matt!" shouted Keir. "Last thing we want is for the Gulden Guards to see us. We'll stand out easily against the snow and there's nowhere to hide."

"I realize that," said Matt, trying to balance while

stopping to take a breather, "but I'm not used to these conditions. It's hot where I come from."

"Don't fret. You've only got another twenty feet."

"Really?" said Matt. But they were still miles from nowhere! When he caught up to Keir he saw he was straddled over a large hole, which seemed to have been tunneled deep in the earth. He was precariously balanced, his legs wide apart and his body bent forward into the hole.

"Take this," said Keir, passing him a dark brown piece of tarp.

"What is it?" asked Matt.

"Just a covering for my valuable possession."

"Which is what, exactly?"

"A canoe," said Keir proudly. "It's just going to be a little difficult getting into it with the river being so high."

"You're not seriously suggesting that we paddle down the Boro-Boro in these conditions, are you?" asked Matt, his voice rising.

"That's what I had in mind," said Keir.

"You must be mad! We'll drown!" Matt shouted. "And what about my computer? I can't risk it getting wet."

"Got a better idea? Our packs are waterproof *and* we wrapped your laptop up in plastic pretty good. It should be okay . . . unless you fall in!"

"If I fall in, I'm dead—never mind the laptop."

"Have faith—I'm good!" Keir grinned at him.

Matt looked at the churning water below. His heart raced. "Can't we keep going on foot?"

"Depends whether you want to get there today or tomorrow! I assume it's today, right?"

Matt sighed. It didn't seem as though he had much choice. But could they even manage to keep the canoe upright? "When you say you're good . . . how good is good?"

"Good enough," answered Keir.

It didn't seem a very reassuring answer.

Keir pulled on the bow of the canoe and hauled it a few feet out of the hole. Then together they tugged on the sides of the canoe, pulling it from its hiding place. Matt had to use all his strength to keep the metal craft from sliding down the bank before they were ready.

"Okay," said Keir breathlessly as he scrambled toward the front of the canoe. "The bank is steep enough that the canoe will slide into the water even with us in it. You ready?"

Matt nodded. "Ready as I'll ever be for this madness."

"On the count of three we'll jump in. One . . . two . . . three! Go!"

Matt leaped into the canoe and fell forward onto the rear seat as they glided down the bank and picked up speed on the snow. He scrambled to sit upright as the bow plunged into the water, sending an icy spray over them both.

The canoe was instantly pushed sideways by the sheer volume of rushing water.

"Grab your paddle and help me!" Keir yelled above the roar of the water. "We've got to turn the bow downstream!"

Matt gripped the sides. Grab his paddle? How? Why had he agreed to go along with this insanity? Just as he bent to retrieve the paddle from under his seat, the canoe tipped to the right, sending him sliding across the seat. He grabbed the side to steady himself. Water poured into the bottom of the boat and sloshed around his feet. Thank goodness his laptop was on his back! He tried again to pull out the paddle.

"Got it!" he said as the canoe pitched again. His head spun. He tried to focus on getting the paddle in the water.

"Paddle on the left side!" shouted Keir. "There are rocks ahead!"

Rocks? We're doomed! We haven't even got control of the boat yet. He paddled furiously, and finally managed to help Keir turn the canoe into the middle of the river.

Black boulders loomed ahead, like gigantic lumps of coal glinting in the sun against the perfect blue sky. Water smashed against the rocks, sending white spray shooting high into the air.

Matt gulped. He was sure the path between the boulders was too narrow for their steering skills. "We'll never make it!" he yelled above the noise of the roaring water. His heart pounded.

"Don't worry. I've done it loads of times before," Keir responded, his voice confident.

But not when the river's been this high, thought Matt, taking several deep breaths. He wanted to close his eyes until it was all over, but that would mean a certain death for both of them. He had to keep calm and work with Keir.

"Three strokes on the left," said Keir. "Now three on the right."

"Got it," said Matt.

Finally they seemed to be working together and making controlled progress. He concentrated on his rhythm rather than on the huge boulders ahead.

"Paddle on your left until I say," said Keir.

"Okay," said Matt. He looked up for a second—and regretted it. Jagged black rocks towered above them on either side. The sight made him stop paddling.

"Why have you stopped? Paddle!" screamed Keir, pulling with all his might.

Matt felt the boat judder and heard the sound of scraping metal beneath him.

"Push off on the left!" screamed Keir again. "We're against the rocks."

Matt's arms ached and his heart seemed to be banging against his chest so hard that he felt as though it might burst. Suddenly the canoe veered to the right and nose-dived through the gap, plummeting down a waterfall. The bow smacked deep in the water, throwing up an enormous wave. Matt tumbled forward, hitting his arm hard against the edge of the boat.

"Ahhh! My arm!" Pain shot through his elbow. When would this nightmare be over?

"Help me! You've got to help me!" screamed Keir. "You can't stop now. There are more rocks ahead!"

Matt dragged himself back onto his seat as the canoe smashed down into the water once again. Trying to ignore his throbbing arm he paddled hard against the violent rapids, listening to Keir's instructions and trying not to focus on the enormous rocks.

Finally the water was calm.

"We're through!" said Keir. "We did it!"

Matt looked up, his hair dripping and water running down his face. Here the river was wide, and the water considerably slower. The rocks were behind them and debris lay in piles along the banks. He took a deep breath and relaxed as the canoe bobbed up and down lightly. "Can't believe we just did that!" he muttered.

"You okay?" asked Keir. He placed his paddle across his knees and turned to look at Matt.

"I'm still here, if that's what you mean," said Matt. "Just got a battered elbow."

"How's the computer?"

"It's still on my back," said Matt. "But there's no telling what damage has been done to it."

"We should be there within an hour. Think you can still paddle?"

"I'll do my best," said Matt, shivering. "The cold will get me before anything else."

"Paddling will keep us warm. If we can meet up with Varak soon, he'll get us some dry clothes."

"*If*? Did you just say *if*?" Matt gulped. "I thought you planned to meet him!"

"Oh, we'll meet him okay—just not sure how long we'll have to wait," Keir reassured.

Matt tried to restrain his anger. "Does he even know

we're coming?"

"No," said Keir, turning away and picking up his paddle again. "I had no way of getting a message to him. I just know where he hangs out."

"But we're soaking wet!" Matt thrust his paddle into the water. "You're joking, right?"

Keir didn't reply.

An icy fear gripped Matt. He'd just survived the treacherous ride down the Boro-Boro River—but now he would freeze to death while waiting for Varak.

* * * * *

A shrill whistle broke into Varl's sleep. He groggily opened his eyes, and just as he realized that it was still dark, the doors flew open and the lights came on. He shielded his eyes with his hand.

"I thought he said our shift began at dawn," grumbled Sarven from the bunk above.

"Up! All of you!" bellowed Captain Culmore. He smacked his whip against the sides of the bunks as he strode down the central aisle. "You've got fifteen minutes to eat breakfast. Now move!"

Gulden Guards entered the room carrying cauldrons and large boxes. Varl swung his legs over the edge of the bed and stood as quickly as he was able. He looked up. The room had suddenly come to life, but Sarven lay in bed stretching lazily.

"Don't be a fool, Sarven," Bronya whispered, as if

reading Varl's mind. "Get up now!"

Culmore paraded to the far end of the bunkhouse, then turned and headed back toward them. Varl winced each time Culmore's whip cut through the air.

"Sarven, get up! I'm begging you. He's coming back this way," Bronya urged again.

Just then Varl saw Sarven propel himself from the upper bunk as if he had suddenly remembered where he was. Culmore had stopped to reprimand someone a few bunks down. His back was turned as he yelled at the cowering man. Varl sighed with relief. Sarven had got up just in time.

Culmore continued toward them. He paused at the foot of Varl's bunk, allowing the whip's six-foot thong to rest on the floor motionless for a few seconds. "Clothing and boots are on the table by the door. Fresh clothing will be delivered at the end of every workday," he said, eyeing Sarven before continuing. "Leave the clothing you're wearing on your bed. Take a backpack from the table. You will be given water and a snack as you enter the mine each day. Is this understood?"

The room was silent.

"Eat. When you hear the next whistle you will line up at the door and your mine guide will take you to shaft 1." With that, Culmore cracked his whip one last time and marched out the door behind him.

Varl sighed with relief. He shook his head at Sarven, who was obviously not an early riser.

"That was close! Did you see the way Culmore looked

at you?" asked Bronya.

"Uh-huh," mumbled Sarven, yawning.

"He's just waiting for you to step out of line. So you'll have to do better than that in the mornings!" chided Varl. He looked around the room. No one moved, as if everyone were paralyzed with fear. "You heard the man! Eat, everyone!" he shouted, clapping his hands twice. "We've got fifteen minutes to eat, and we'll need food if we're going to survive a day's work down in the mine."

The chatter resumed. Everyone headed to the end of the room, where piles of clothes and steaming cauldrons had been placed on a large table.

Varl headed to the clothing table first. He fingered the red lightweight linen shirts and pants with draw string waistbands. "Not bad."

"Not bad? They're ugly and huge!" said Bronya. "Even the small size will swamp me. And just look at the huge rubber boots—they come up to my knees!"

"Don't complain. You'll need all of it," said Sarven, leaning over her shoulder. He reached for a medium-sized set. "No way could I have worked in my thick clothes. The heat would have killed me."

"The heat might still kill you," said Bronya in a sarcastic tone.

Varl pulled on his new outfit and placed his own clothing in a neat pile at the foot of his bed. "I guess they want to keep us alive and working for as long as they can. Let's see what's for breakfast." He waddled across the room in the heavy boots.

Sarven beat him to the second table. "I'm starving," he said, finally showing some life. But as he excitedly removed the lid from one of the cauldrons, his face quickly changed to a look of sheer disgust. "What's this slop? It smells horrible!"

"I believe it's porridge," said Varl, sniffing the rising steam. "It smells okay to me."

"You think?" Bronya picked up the ladle and scooped up a portion of the thick oatmeal stodge. It plopped in one lump into her bowl. "Yuk!" she groaned.

"Just eat it," said Varl. "We need food, no matter what it tastes like."

Varl sat down at one of the tables. He imagined his favorite food from the kitchens of Zaul as he swallowed the first tasteless spoonful. "Eat the lot," he mumbled in between bites. "We've got to keep our strength to survive." He scraped his bowl clean and urged Bronya and Sarven to do the same.

The second whistle sounded. Varl grabbed a green canvas backpack and beckoned Bronya and Sarven to join him in the line, wondering which of the mean-faced Gulden Guards from the night before was to be their mine guide.

The door opened, sending in a rush of freezing air. A thin man, dressed in a thick coat and a knitted black hat embroidered with HJG, stepped into the room. He smiled in a forced way and said quietly, "Everyone follow me, please."

Varl was taken aback. He had expected more

smacking of whips and Gulden Guards in black leather, not a feeble old man saying *please*. He wrapped his arms tightly across his body in an effort to keep warm as the man led them across the snow-covered road and between two other bunkhouses. His mind began to churn. The mine guide would be a valuable resource if he could just get him to talk.

Varl moved alongside the mine guide, leaving Bronya and Sarven walking behind. "You been here long?" he asked.

"HJG? Yeah, a long time," the mine guide answered.

"How many years?"

"Too long. Three years of working down in the mine earned me this job, and I've been doing this for a year now."

"Four years. I've been told that most people don't survive two."

"You were told right."

"You must know a lot about the mine and the equipment," said Varl. "Bet you know where the shafts go, how many Gulden Guards work each shift and all about these Gnasher things."

The mine guide turned and scowled at him. "You think I'm stupid or something? Are you *trying* to get me killed?"

"I don't understand," said Varl, trying to sound innocent. "What did I say?"

The mine guide gave him a bewildered look. Varl did his best to maintain an expression of naivete.

"I was just interested, nothing more," said Varl. "Is

there a crime in that?"

The mine guide snorted. "Ask no questions and do what you're told. That's my advice. Then you'll survive and get a better life, like me."

"A better life?" Varl shot back. "This? A mine guide?"

"It's a lot better than what you'll be doing today! I've got one more year and then I'm out of here. So stay out of my business," he snapped, striding ahead.

Varl fell back in step with Sarven and Bronya. "I think I was a bit too obvious," he admitted. "I think I just scared him off. I'll have to find someone else who'll give us information."

Sarven chuckled. "Shame, old man. He was probably your best bet."

"Thanks for the sympathy," Varl said sarcastically. "That's what I was afraid of."

The mine guide led them along a row of bunkhouses—row upon row upon row, equally spaced apart, every one exactly the same. Varl quickly estimated that there were at least fifty bunkhouses in this area of the complex. That was a lot of prisoners. He looked around. There were a lot of armed Gulden Guards too. Overpowering them would not be an option.

Varl studied the buildings, which rested on wooden supports at least two feet off the ground. Underneath, plumbing pipes entered the bunkhouses from the street. He looked to the roofs. Was there a security system of some kind? Although he couldn't see any telltale signs, surely there had to be cameras trained on each bunkhouse. He'd have to find out.

The noise of mine machinery grew louder as they turned the corner and walked across the main square. Without the protection of the bunkhouses the chilly wind cut through his flimsy clothing, so Varl focused on the entrance to mine shaft 1 in the distance.

"This is the pit-head," said Sarven. "It's where all the machinery is housed and where all the miners enter and leave the mine."

"And what's that?" asked Bronya, pointing to a tall metal tower.

"That's called the headgear," said Sarven. "It supports the two winding wheels. As the wheels turn, the miners' cage is brought up and down."

"Cage?" said Bronya.

"Yeah. It's like an open elevator with metal bars all round."

Varl looked at the enormous wheels that turned slowly at the top of the structure. Apart from the huge roaring fans at the base of the pit-head, this could have been a coal mine.

As they walked through the winding house Varl took in as much detail of the winding machinery as he could. He sketched in his mind the layout of the engines, cylinder drums and the huge winding ropes, knowing the information might be useful. It was a twin headgear system, which meant that one cage would be coming to the surface as another was lowered.

"Line up here," announced the mine guide, pointing at

a white line painted across the concrete floor. Six armed Gulden Guards hovered nearby, making their presence felt. "You will be fitted with equipment. Put it on and move forward to the cage."

Varl was handed a hard hat. It had a light on the front connected by a thick black lead to a heavy battery pack, which he belted around his waist. Inwardly he groaned. The extra weight would just add to the difficulty of working in the heat.

He stared at the huge cage in front of him, which had just reached the surface carrying the prisoners from the last shift. Through the metal bars he saw a crowd of dirty, exhausted people. He gulped. Soon he would be lowered deep into the Earth and there would be nothing but darkness and heat for eight hours.

A buzzer sounded. The mine guide then drew back the doors. Varl winced as they screeched open. The prisoners staggered out of the cage and toward them, heads lowered, filthy, sweaty and obviously exhausted. Varl looked at their solemn faces and wondered how he would feel at three o'clock when his shift ended.

"Move forward!" ordered one of the Gulden Guards, prodding Varl in the shoulder with the butt of his rifle.

"No! Hold it!" snapped a high-pitched scratchy voice from behind.

The guard in front of the cage instantly raised his ST29 to prevent Varl from entering. "Turn around," growled the guard.

Varl turned and found himself face to face with

Bronya. The color had drained from her cheeks, her eyes were wide and she clenched her teeth and fists as if trying to control her anger. It was as if she were frozen on the spot.

Behind Bronya a small man in bright green medieval attire was striding to the front of the line, his golden cloak flapping behind him in the wind.

"All bow for Horando Javeer, Keeper of the Colony of Javeer!" shouted the guard, pushing Varl's head forward with his rifle.

A chill ran down Varl's spine. He briefly bent at the waist and then dared to peek at the small straggly-haired man dwarfed by the Gulden Guards on either side.

So this was the man himself. Varl tried hard to conceal a smile. Javeer looked more like a court jester than a fearsome leader.

Horando Javeer stopped in front of the cage and looked straight into Bronya's eyes.

"*Miss* Bronya Logan," he said slowly and emphatically. "We meet again. I am sure that by now you are regretting your decision not to cooperate with me."
Bronya's lips curled into a sneer but she said nothing.

"I am told by my informant that your brother and the stranger from Gova have disappeared from the Dark End. It seems that they talked of a rescue mission to get you out of here. I can see that stupidity runs in your family."

Bronya's sneer developed a hint of a smile, and Varl's heart began to race as he realized what Javeer had said. The stranger from Gova had to be Matt.

"*It seems* that your informants are the stupid ones if they don't know where my brother is. So now you really do have something to worry about," she replied.

Horando Javeer raised his hand and smacked her hard across the cheek. "You will address me as Keeper!" he shouted.

Bronya barely flinched. She glared at him, her lips pursed defiantly together.

Horando Javeer hit her hard a second time.

This time she yelped.

"You will address me as Keeper!" he screamed in her face.

Sarven stepped forward in a protective stance but immediately one of the Gulden Guards pulled him back.

Varl watched with horror as blood poured from Bronya's lower lip.

"Keeper," she finally muttered, raising her hand to dab her mouth.

"Good," said Javeer. "Now that we have that settled, I will make you a deal. You will give me information about the stranger and his computer, and in exchange I will spare your brother's life."

Varl gulped. He suddenly felt hot and dizzy. Would Bronya turn in Matt to save her brother?

"No deal, Keeper," spat Bronya.

Javeer grabbed Bronya's short hair and yanked her towards him. "Protecting your brother is one thing, but loyalty to a complete stranger is foolish!" His words were loaded with ridicule. "Do you really think that your brother could get you out of here? He will be shot on sight!"

"Your word means nothing, Keeper!" said Bronya through clenched teeth. "If I give you what you want, you will still send my brother down the mine. So why should I help you? I have nothing to gain."

Javeer released his grip on Bronya's hair and shoved her backwards into Sarven. "We'll soon see about that!" he hissed. "Culmore is out looking for your brother and the stranger from Gova as we speak. They can't hide from my Gulden Guards for long. We'll have them before nightfall."

Bronya tipped back her head and laughed defiantly. "You obviously don't know my brother. He's been hiding from your Gulden Guards for several years and they haven't caught him yet. They're useless!"

Javeer colored instantly. He stiffened, anger burning in his eyes. Varl silently cheered. Bronya had humiliated Javeer.

"Put everyone in bunkhouse 157 on heavy labor," Javeer ordered, his voice quaking. "Send them all to the pit bottom. We'll see if Bronya Logan changes her tune tomorrow."

There were gasps from the other prisoners.

"I'll tell Culmore to double the guard on each shift," he shouted as he walked away, his cape billowing behind.

There was silence momentarily. Even the Gulden Guards on duty seemed taken aback by Javeer's outburst, but then they quickly got back to the business at hand.

"Your lunch," one of the guards grunted, handing Varl a canteen of water and a brown bag. He struggled to put it in his backpack as he was pushed forward into the far corner of the cage. Sarven and Bronya followed and stood in silence next to him. He was proud of Bronya. She was one brave young lady.

"Move to the back," shouted the guard. "We've got to get fifteen of you in here."

Varl winced as his right arm was shoved against the metal bars of the cage, and again as the man in front of him stepped back onto his big toe. The cage was so packed he could barely breathe. His lunch in his backpack wouldn't be in a fit state to eat, that was for sure.

The last person was squeezed in and the door closed. The machinery whined and the steel cage shuddered. Seconds later they were thrust into darkness, descending fast. Varl guessed they were traveling at least forty miles per hour. He counted. Ten seconds, eleven, twelve . . . forty . . . forty-five . . . one hundred . . . one hundred and thirty . . . .. How deep were they going?

The cage finally slowed and jolted to a stop. Varl wasn't sure which hit him first—the putrid dank smell or the sweltering heat.

Gnashers? Ha! The pit bottom was bad enough!

He turned on his headlamp and followed Bronya and Sarven into the dark tunnel, bracing himself for the work ahead. One thought comforted him: Javeer had confirmed that Matt and Keir Logan were on their way to rescue them. Matt would need a lot of help from the inside if he were to outsmart Horando Javeer. Varl had plenty to do.

Chapter 11

Matt had no idea where they were heading. It was nearly dark, they were deep in a pine forest, and he'd never been so cold in his entire life. Keir wouldn't give him any clues as to their destination, saying it was for the best, in case they were captured by Gulden Guards.

"K-K-Keir, I c-c-c-an't go m-m-m-uch farther," said Matt, feeling like a wimp. "I c-c-can't feel my fingers or toes."

"Don't worry, we'll be in front of a fire within a few minutes. Just a short distance more, I promise. Okay?"

"Okay," muttered Matt, wondering what choice he had but to continue.

They had walked at least a mile since leaving the treacherous Boro-Boro River. Keir had chosen a place surrounded by trees and thick shrubs to come ashore. They had dragged the canoe out of the water and up the icy bank, and then left it well hidden beneath a layer of brown needles, cones and leaves.

Matt suddenly saw a glimmer of yellow light through the trees. Was his mind playing tricks on him? No, there *was* a cottage in the distance. He could see it more clearly now. His spirits lifted. Perhaps he wouldn't die of cold after all. Smoke rose from a chimney on the roof. He could almost feel the warmth of the fire already.

"We're here," announced Keir.

"Where *is* here?"

"Varak's cottage. Well, his aunt's cottage, actually."

"And we're just going to knock on her door and hope she'll invite us in?" asked Matt in disbelief.

"Exactly," said Keir confidently as he approached the door and knocked loudly.

A short dumpy woman with gray hair, rosy cheeks and a wide smile greeted them. "Keir Logan!" she exclaimed, pulling him quickly inside. "You poor thing—you're frozen!"

"This is my friend, Matt Hammond," said Keir, heading straight for the roaring fire. "Matt, this is Mrs. Morsova, Varak's aunt."

"Nice to meet you, ma'am," stammered Matt, hesitating in the doorway.

"Don't just stand there, young man! Come in! Come in!" she said, pulling Matt after Keir. "What happened to you both?"

"A canoe trip down the Boro-Boro," said Keir matter-of-factly.

"At this time of year and in these conditions?" she replied, shaking her head in disbelief. "You must be mad!"

"It's an emergency," said Matt, still shaking with cold. "We had no choice."

She frowned. "Well, get those soaking clothes off right now and wrap yourselves in the blankets on the sofa—you'll die of pneumonia! I'll be back with towels and you can tell me what I can do to help you with this emergency."

With that she left the room.

"Hope my laptop survived," said Matt, letting the sopping backpack slip gently from his shoulders.

"Get yourself warm and dry before you worry about it."

"Sorry, can't," said Matt. "Cold as I am, I've got to take a look. I've been worrying about it all day." He placed the backpack on the floor and quickly removed his laptop, still wrapped in plastic. "It looks okay," he said, feeling very relieved. "Can't see any water inside the plastic."

"Good news. Now get in front of this fire."

"You didn't tell me you knew Varak's aunt," said Matt, eagerly peeling his dripping jeans down his legs. He was beginning to feel badly for doubting Keir.

"Met her last year. Varak brought me here. She said I could come here if I ever needed help." Keir dumped his wet clothes in a pile and grabbed the blankets off the sofa. "Here, want one?"

Matt nodded. "Thanks. I can't believe we get to wait for Varak in comfort. The way you were talking, I thought we'd be freezing in a barn tonight."

"Give me some credit," laughed Keir. "I couldn't exactly go into details while we were battling down the Boro-Boro. Besides, the less you knew, the better—in case we were captured by Gulden Guards on the way. She's a great cook, by the way."

"And boy, am I hungry," said Matt sitting down directly

in front of the blazing logs. "All that exercise has certainly given me an appetite.

"Here you are. Dry your hair," said Mrs. Morsova, returning with two large towels.

"Thanks, ma'am. This is really good of you," said Matt, reaching for a towel. "I was beginning to think I'd die of cold out there."

"No problem. Besides, it's nice to have the company. Now what would you two young men like to eat? I've got some potato soup. How's that sound to start with?"

"Sounds like a feast," said Keir.

She smiled. "Good. I'll be right back and then you can fill me in on your troubles."

Mrs. Morsova left the room, and Matt looked around. Compared with the basic furnishings he'd seen in Keir's home, this house was luxurious.

"How come she has so much furniture and food compared to everyone else?" asked Matt.

"The Gulden Guards probably don't know she's here, and even if they did, they probably wouldn't bother her. They don't consider her a threat—an elderly woman living on her own several miles from the East End. But she's self sufficient and very capable. She grows her own vegetables and hunts small animals. She's got wood from the forest, which is of course getting smaller by the day as everyone in the East End cuts down the trees for fuel."

"Where's Mr. Morsova?"

"Dead," said Keir bluntly. "Which is one reason she can be trusted."

"The Gulden Guards?"

"You guessed it. Mr. Morsova worked for the Underground and was caught one night at a council meeting in the East End. He was sentenced to the mine and died four years ago."

"No wonder Varak hates Horando Javeer."

"Yeah. Thanks to Javeer he's lost two brothers and an uncle, and his third brother is still a prisoner at the mine."

"So when will we see Varak?"

"He comes here to see his aunt at least once a week."

Matt frowned. "But we don't have time to sit here and wait for him to come—it could be days." He studied Keir's face. There was something Keir wasn't telling him. "What's going on, Keir Logan? I can't believe that you're prepared to waste time when your sister's life is on the line—not after the canoe trip you've just put me through to get here in a hurry."

Keir smiled as Mrs. Morsova came back into the room with two steaming bowls. "Don't worry, my friend. Mrs. Morsova has a method of contacting Varak when needed."

"I can have him here by noon tomorrow," she said with a knowing smile. "So why don't you tell me what's happened and I'll see what I can do."

* * * * *

"Told you so," said Jake. "I'm the man! Told you I'd get them down that river in one piece." He tipped back his head and roared with laughter.

Targon sighed. That perilous canoe trip had been almost too much for him to bear. He wondered how Matt was feeling after his death-defying journey. "Yeah, you're the man," he repeated quietly. "Now that we've completed *that* task, let's move on to the next."

"We still don't have any weapons," said Jake with a yawn, swiveling his chair around to face Targon. "That's *got* to be the next task."

"I told you before—we can't get weapons until we know what enemy we're fighting," Targon said. "We've got to find out who the two Keepers are first, and which one we have to destroy."

"Aww, this is such a naf game!" said Jake. "We've been playing for over an hour and we still don't have any weapons. I hate games without weapons. Where's that dorky brother of mine? How long can it take him to throw on some clothes and get back down here?"

Targon's heart raced. "I thought you wanted to beat this level before he came back."

"That's before I found out what a boring game this is," Jake snorted. "Matt might as well play. I'm about ready to quit."

Targon winced. Jake couldn't quit! What would happen to Matt if he did? He had to keep Jake involved in the game. "Zang it! Forget Matt," he urged. "Let's show him what *you and I* can do."

"Zang it? That's a new one," said Jake, showing sudden interest. "Where'd ya hear that?"

Targon gulped. "Er. . . this game. On Level 1, in the Kingdom of Zaul. Everyone's playing this Keeper game and everyone's saying 'Zang it!' at school."

Jake grimaced. "They are? Well, zang it, then! Let's get some weapons. We know Hornado Javeer is a Keeper. He's taken over Boro and has made himself the Keeper of the Colony of Javeer. He's making the people work as slaves, killing them down in his gold mine. What more information do we need? He's got to be the Keeper we want. Let's blast him out of the game and then maybe the game won't be so boring!"

Targon felt as though he were hitting his head against a brick wall. "And what if he isn't the *right* Keeper? Or what if blasting him out of the game isn't the answer? Do you want to lose Level 4 because you didn't wait for all of the clues?"

"Look. You read the rhyme the same as I did," Jake snapped. "I thought you were smart. It said, *'One will prove a useful friend, make a pact and then defend.'* You don't think we're going to be defending Horando Javeer, do you? I sure don't."

"But it can't be as easy as you said," retorted Targon. "I'm telling you, the game often has surprises. Let's not give up and take the easy way out now."

Jake tipped back on his chair, stretched his arms above his head and stared at the screen. He looked bored.

Targon's heart was pounding against his chest. *Please don't quit on me*, he thought. "Come on, Jake.

Click on the menu. Let's see what our options are," he said, praying that something would be interesting enough to keep Jake from leaving. Not everything exciting had to be about weapons! Hadn't that adrenaline-pumping canoe ride been enough?

Targon struggled to read the list of options on the menu. Just as he was about to suggest trying Number 1, 'Maps,' Jake pressed Number 7, 'Weapons.'

"Why did you go and do that?" Targon screamed at him.

Jake shrugged. "Sorry, couldn't resist. This game needs some action, fast."

"We've had plenty of action!" Targon shot back. "That canoe ride was action!"

"Hey, kid. Chill, man. It's just a game. Don't get so upset!"

Targon wished that were true. But he certainly couldn't tell Jake it wasn't just a game, could he? "Well, what's done is done," he said glumly.

"Shall I put it on audio?" asked Jake.

"Sure," said Targon. "Let's hear the rhyme."

The picture darkened so much that Targon had to strain to see what was on the screen. Long low tunnels wound their way deeper and deeper into the Earth, and only dim light flickered against the walls and roof.

"Mines, I think," said Jake.

Targon shuddered. "Which means that when we chose the canoe ride to Horando Javeer's gold mine we were on the right track. The mine is where we are meant to be."

A deep voice growled the rhyme.

> Rebuilding Boro is the key
> Destroy the pit-head and you *won't* succeed
> Know the Gnashers if you dare
> Use technology, not weapons, to prepare
> With their Keeper fight a common foe
> Or your enemy's greed is sure to grow
> Stop his source with a careful plan
> Destroy the mine and not the man.

"I don't get it. No weapons?" snarled Jake. He slammed his hand down on the desk next to the computer. "How can you defeat an enemy without weapons?"

Targon smiled. "We've done it before," he mumbled.

"Who's done it before?"

"Oh, Matt and I, on Level 2 of this game. We didn't fire one shot and yet we defeated Nonius Balbus in *Keeper of the Realm.*"

"How?" asked Jake, his eyebrows coming together in that now-familiar manner.

"Ingenuity and well thought-out plans," said Targon, feeling very proud of what they'd done in that level. "Weapons aren't always the answer."

Jake sighed. "So you keep telling me. But it's pretty boring without them."

"Oh, our enemy will have plenty of weapons, for sure," said Targon, worrying that Jake might quit if weapons didn't play a major part in the game. "We've seen the Gulden Guards walking around with whips and ST29s. It won't be boring if we have to go up against them!"

"Right, if you say so," said Jake. He scowled. "Though I don't know how we can go up against ST29s without weapons to combat them."

"We've just got to be one step ahead," said Targon.

"Okay. So what do you make of the rhyme? I'm not very good at solving puzzles."

"Well, it does look as though the Keeper we have to destroy *is* Horando Javeer."

"Told you so," said Jake with a mocking smile.

"But we're not blasting him out of the game. It says to destroy the mine, not the man.   You can destroy someone's business, someone's home and someone's life. You don't have to physically destroy the person. Destroying the mine would destroy Horando Javeer. It would cut off his supply of gold and just maybe he'd leave."

"Yeah, agreed. But who are the Gnashers?"

Targon shook his head. "Not sure at the moment, but with that name they don't sound too friendly."

Jake pointed to the last two lines of the rhyme on the screen. "Anyway, you missed this bit—it says if we destroy the pit-head we won't succeed."

"I didn't miss it. I just don't get it," said Targon. "Aren't the pithead and the mine the same thing? How confusing is that?"

"You obviously don't know anything about mining,"

said Jake. "The pithead is the entrance to the mine above the ground, and the actual mine is below ground."

"Oh," said Targon, impressed by Jake's sudden show of knowledge. "How did you know that?"

Jake shrugged. "School. Go figure. Guess I must have listened to something our naf history teacher said."

"Guess you must have," said Targon. He hadn't yet figured Jake out. One minute he came off as tough and downright dumb, but the next minute he seemed almost nice and reasonably intelligent.

"So what should we do?" said Jake, bringing Targon back from his thoughts.

"Get Matt and Keir to the mine," said Targon, knowing it couldn't possibly be that simple.

"I know, I know," grumbled Jake. "The rhyme says to make a careful plan. Since we've been told we can't use weapons, I suppose you want me to press Number 1, '*Maps*.'"

Targon smiled. He was right. Jake wasn't so dumb after all.

Chapter 12

Matt sat in front of the fire waiting for Varak to arrive. He reached for his laptop, reopened *'Weapons'* and read the rhyme a second time. Something was wrong with his computer game, which was really worrying. Even though he could open up the menu, click on any of the icons and pull up the instructions, it was as if someone had beaten him to it every step of the way. According to his computer log, *'Weapons'* had been opened less than one hour before. Someone else was playing the game. The game instructions had even stated that there were two players this time. But who was the second player? He shook his head and sighed. He just couldn't figure it out.

"I don't know what your problem is—it seems pretty obvious to me," said Keir, sprawled across the carpet next to him. "The rhyme's just confirmed what we'd already worked out. Two Keepers, one is our ally and the other is to be destroyed. The one we're supposed to destroy has to be Horando Javeer. He's greedy and he's taken over the gold mine. He has to be stopped so that we can rebuild Boro. I'm sure we'll find out how to get rid of him when we find Bronya and Varl."

If only it were that easy, thought Matt. At least Keir

had the same objectives at the end of the day. The game rules said to locate and destroy the Keeper and free the people, which was exactly what Keir wanted, too.

"*Know the Gnashers if you dare,*" read Matt. "Why won't you discuss this part of the rhyme with me?"

Keir shrugged. "What's to discuss? The rhyme's got to be wrong. There's no way that we could get to know the Gnashers and make them our ally against Horando. I'm sorry, but that's a hard one for me or anyone from Boro to swallow."

"Well, what are they? I mention Gnashers to anyone and they clam up and refuse to talk. All I know is that they supposedly live in the gold mine and supposedly attack humans."

"Not supposedly—they do! I've seen the proof. Gulden Guards with hundreds of tiny teeth marks all over them. What a gruesome way to die! Yet *you* want us to befriend and work with these . . . these things?"

"Okay, then. Tell me what Gnashers look like. How do we talk to them?"

Keir sat up and warmed his hands in front of the flames. "Don't know how they communicate. Only one or two people have survived to pass on any information. I do know they can fly. I've heard they're about the size of small bats and they're golden and metallic looking."

"Are these Gnasher things actually living beings?"

"Well, what else would they be?"

Matt thought of the Cybergons in Level 1 of his game. They weren't living beings of any kind but they'd been brutal.

"Varak should be here within the hour," said Keir, obviously wanting to change the subject.

"Great. I got a good night's sleep for the first time in ages and now I'm ready to get to work. I was so surprised yesterday when Mrs. Morsova said she used carrier pigeons to contact Varak. Those birds are fantastic! Well, that is, if they really do deliver her messages."

"She's used them to contact Varak hundreds of times before. Don't worry. They're reliable. I'm sure he'll be here in time for lunch, just as she promised."

There was a loud knock on the front door.

"Bet that's him now," said Keir.

Mrs. Morsova hurried from the kitchen, drying her hands on her white apron. She glanced around the room nervously and motioned to Matt and Keir to pick up their belongings and hide behind the sofa.

Matt felt his pulse quicken, more from excitement than nerves. Finally Varak was arriving and he couldn't wait to meet him. But why was Mrs. Morsova so anxious? Hurriedly he gathered up his bedding and his laptop, and scuttled behind the sofa. As he tried to make himself comfortable on the cold floor, he heard Varak's aunt draw in a deep breath and open the heavy door.

She gasped. "Er . . .Gulden Guards," she said loudly. "What can I do for you gentlemen?"

"I'm Captain Culmore. We're looking for two young men who are plotting to free prisoners from the Horando Javeer Gold Mine. We found a canoe hidden not a mile from here. Has anyone asked for help or shelter in the last twenty-four hours?"

"Er, no. No one's been here in days," replied Varak's aunt.

Matt froze. He stared into Keir's panic-stricken eyes.

"Ma'am, I'm sure you know the penalty for harboring enemies of Horando Javeer."

"Yes, sir, indeed I do." Her voice shook noticeably. "Are these young men armed and dangerous?"

Culmore chuckled. "Hardly. They're just a minor problem. Mind if I look around for a minute?"

"No, not at all. Come in. Be my guest."

Matt's stomach churned as he heard the sound of heavy boots on the floor. Had he left anything lying around? His backpack! He'd put it under the little log table by the side of the sofa. What if the Captain noticed it? He and Varak would both be arrested, that's what. Could he reach it? He stuck his hand out from behind the sofa and felt under the little table until his fingers touched the strap. Slowly, gently, he began to drag it toward himself, inch by inch.

Matt heard Culmore sniff the air. "You cooking for someone, Ma'am?"

Culmore was standing right next to the sofa! Matt gulped. He released his grip on the pack and pulled back his hand, praying that Culmore wouldn't look down.

"Oh, no. Just preparing my lunch. Would you like some rabbit stew? I always make plenty so that it will last me all week."

Culmore cleared his throat. "It smells good, but I've a job to do."

"Well perhaps next time you come this way you'll stop by," said Mrs. Morsova in a courteous tone.

Culmore grunted his appreciation. "Remember ma'am, traitors are not tolerated. The mine isn't far from here, so I know you are aware of the consequences."

"Indeed, sir."

"We'll be watching."

"Yes, Captain Culmore. Thank you for stopping by."

Matt heard the door close, then . . . nothing. He listened for sounds that would indicate they had left the property, but there were none. He dared not move.

Several minutes passed before Keir whispered, "Have they gone?"

"You can come out," said Mrs. Morsova. "But stay on the floor and away from the windows."

"Well, we're in real trouble now," said Matt, peering around the sofa. "If the Gulden Guards are watching your cottage we'll never get away from here, and Varak will be caught as soon as he shows up."

Mrs. Morsova grinned. "Don't worry about Varak. There are ways."

"You knew it wasn't Varak at the door," said Matt, trying to piece together what had just happened. "How?"

"Varak won't come through the front door." She broke into a wide, open smile. "In fact, I hear him arriving now."

But there isn't a back door, thought Matt.

A rugged profile walked in from the kitchen. "Hi, Aunt

Leila! Hope I got here fast enough."

"Varak! Timed perfectly. Good thing you didn't get here any earlier."

"Gulden Guards?" said Varak, ducking and looking to the windows.

She nodded. "'Fraid so. Best you stay low for the moment." She bent and planted a huge kiss on his cheek.

"Your note was more cryptic than usual but I got the meaning." He unfolded the tiny piece of paper that she had secured to a ring around the pigeon's foot. 'I'm not well' is our usual code that you need me, and I guessed that 'Beware, the river crossing is high' means that Keir Logan is here?"

Keir laughed and crawled out from behind the sofa. "Great going, Varak."

"Good to see you, Keir," said Varak, shuffling over to him and slapping him on the back.

"This is my friend, Matt Hammond. We need your help urgently."

Matt moved into view. "Thanks for coming so quickly."

"Pleased to meet you, Matt," said Varak in a voice that conveyed some suspicion.

The wild-haired young man reminded Matt a little of Gorbun, but he had an easy, friendly smile and exuded an air of confidence. Somehow Matt just knew that Varak would be able to help him find Varl.

"Hungry?" asked Mrs. Morsova.

"Aunt Leila," said Varak. "You're not going to wait on us. I don't want you worn out."

"Nonsense! You've come all this way so you must eat something. I like to cook for you, you know that."

"Is that your famous rabbit stew I can smell?"

"Indeed it is," she said. "Bet you peeked in the pot as you came through the kitchen!"

Varak grinned. "Caught me!" he teased.

"Give me fifteen minutes and you'll have a good hot meal to warm you. Better get back into the basement in case Captain Culmore decides to pay us another visit."

Basement? thought Matt. *So that was how Varak got here without being seen.* He grabbed his laptop and slithered across the floor into the kitchen after the others. Mrs. Morsova had removed the red woven rug from under the kitchen table and was holding open a trap door.

"Thanks, Aunt Leila," said Varak. He scrambled down the wooden ladder, followed immediately by Keir.

Matt descended quickly after them. He jumped off the bottom rung and squinted to see in the dark basement. A single oil lamp suspended from the center of the ceiling over a rustic wooden table dimly lit the small space. The earthen walls had been reinforced roughly with planks of timber. Leading off from the far side of the room was a narrow tunnel.

Varak smiled proudly. "My Uncle Gregori ran the East End Underground Council and this is where they met. They would arrive through that tunnel. There are actually two rooms down here." He pointed to a door near the ladder. "Sometimes members would sleep here."

"Are the rooms still used by the Underground?" asked

Matt.

Varak shook his head. "No. When Uncle Gregori and some of the Underground Council were captured, the others changed their meeting place for safety." He pulled up a chair from the side of the room. "Sit down, both of you, and tell me what I can do to help."

Matt eagerly pulled up a chair around the table in the center and listened as Keir recounted how Bronya had been captured and sent to the mine. Varak's face became serious and thoughtful.

"We're so lucky to have Matt," said Keir. "He's a runner from Gova, sent on a mission to help us defeat Hornado Javeer and reclaim Boro."

"A runner from Gova? Really?" said Varak, his voice skeptical.

"He came three days ago with two other runners," Keir continued. "I just happened to bump into him on the street after a raid by the Gulden Guards."

"You just happened to bump into him," repeated Varak, frowning.

"Targon, who's our age, seems to have completely vanished," said Matt, ignoring Varak's obvious distrust. "Varl, an elderly man who's a scientist, has been captured by the Gulden Guards and is probably also at the mine. My computer holds all kinds of information that has guided us on our mission so far and will help us to rid Boro of Javeer."

"Computer?" said Varak, his tone now verging on disbelief.

"Right here," said Matt, sliding his laptop across the table toward Varak. "I'll show you how it works later."

"So if you have all this information to defeat Javeer stored on your computer, why do you need me?" Varak's voice dripped with doubt.

Matt knew he had to convince Varak to help. He had failed to convince the Dark End Underground Council and he couldn't fail a second time. "Look, Varak, I know that Javeer has spies everywhere, so it is dangerous for you to trust a stranger. But surely you can see that if I worked for Javeer I'd have already turned Keir over to him."

"Perhaps you're just gathering information so that the whole Underground network can be destroyed in one go," said Varak, raising his eyebrows.

"You don't really believe that," said Matt. "Your gut instinct is telling you that I'm one of the good guys—I can see it in your eyes."

"Perhaps," said Varak, studying him.

"I don't know what proof I can give you, except to show you my computer. I must find my friends in order to complete this mission successfully."

"So, what's in it for you?" pressed Varak. "Why come all this way from Gova to risk your life for the people of Boro?"

Matt had to think fast. It was a good question and one that Keir hadn't thought to ask him. Varak was smart. Matt couldn't tell him the truth—that this was all just a computer game. Even Varl wasn't convinced of that, after completing three levels in the *Keeper of the Kingdom* game.

"I'm risking my life for the people of Gova, not for the people of Boro," said Matt with conviction. "Do you have any idea what it was like living under the rule of the Vorgs? It's not something we ever want to experience again. The Govan Reistance worked hard to get rid of the Vorgs and now the people of Gova are frightened by Horando Javeer on their borders. He's a man who at any minute might get even more greedy and decide to march into Gova."

Varak nodded, and seemed to accept his explanation. "Hmmm. I can understand Govan fears after what you've been through."

"All I'm asking is that you get us into the gold mine," implored Matt.

"*Into* the gold mine?" said Varak, choking on his words. "What kind of idiot are you? Now I do believe you. Only a fool would want to go *into* the mine when everyone else is trying to get out!"

"Our plan is not only to rescue Bronya and Varl, but also to destroy the mine," said Keir.

Varak laughed. "Now you really have got my attention! Just how do you think you're going to do all that?"

"We're at the early stages of planning, which is why we need you. How many Gulden Guards are at the mine? What weapons do they have? Should we go through the gates or under the fence—which is the weakest point?"

Keir shook his head. "You'll never get over or under the fence, or past the towers and all of the guards that are on duty. The gates and the fence are electrified, and both have barbed wire on top. No one's ever managed to escape from the mine but many have died trying."

"So, you're saying we can't get in?" asked Keir.

"I'm saying there's no way through the gates or over the fence."

"There's always a way to get in," said Matt, sensing that Varak was holding something back.

Varak drew a deep breath. "True. Just not that way."

"Then how?" asked Matt, leaning forward across the table eagerly.

"It's only a theory I have . . . something I've been thinking about," said Varak in a whisper.

"Go on," said Keir, leaning so far forward he was almost off his chair. "Speak up! Tell us!"

"I've studied old maps of the area and I'm pretty certain that you can get into the mine shafts through the back of Boro-Boro Mountain."

"How?" asked Matt.

"Gold has been mined in Boro since long before Javeer arrived. Javeer closed the entrances on the north side of the mountain and concentrated on creating a town and excavating the shafts on the south side. On the maps it looks like two of the old shafts on the north side join up underground with shafts that Javeer uses now."

"Do you think that they're still open?"

"No way of knowing until you get down the shafts," said Varak. "They may have been blocked off or they might have caved in."

Matt got to his feet. "That's not going to stop us. We'll take some explosives and digging equipment with us. Don't you see? This is perfect. This is the last thing that Javeer will expect. There'll be no guards to deal with *and* we can destroy the mine from inside."

"But you'll still have the Gnashers to deal with. That's your real problem."

"No, trust me, the Gnashers will help us," said Matt with confidence.

Varak's eyes nearly flew from their sockets. "What did you just say?"

"That the Gnashers will help us."

"Mad! You really are mad! Keir, you can't seriously want to go along with this idiot. Where does he get such information?"

Keir shrugged. "His laptop. And sure, I'll go along with him. I've got to get Bronya out of there."

Varak grunted. "Some of what you said makes sense, but some of it is utter stupidity. Let's forget the problem of the Gnashers for a moment. How are you going to destroy the mines when several hundred people work there twenty-four hours a day? You've got to get all of them out of there before you can set off explosives. Then there's another problem. You can't carry explosives with you because they're so unstable, so you'll have to steal some when you get there. Then, what's the guarantee that you'll do enough damage to the mine so that Javeer will give up and leave Boro?"

"None," said Matt. "There's no guarantee. But as I said

to the Dark End Underground Council, what have you done to get rid of Javeer in the last twenty years?"

"You actually said that to the council?" said Varak, a stunned look on his face.

Matt nodded. "And they didn't like it."

"I'm not surprised. You were criticizing their efforts."

"And so I should! No one has tried to defeat Javeer since he marched in and took over Boro. For twenty years there's been nothing but talk and planning and setting up the network, and meanwhile Javeer has destroyed everything in sight. The people of Boro are getting desperate. They're hungry and cold—you both know that! I'll bet you anything that with just one successful attack, everyone will have the courage to rebel. Javeer won't be expecting this!"

Varak was silent.

Matt turned to appeal to Keir. "Don't you see? Varak has given us the perfect way into the mine. Isn't it worth a try?"

"Oh, you needn't convince me," said Keir. "I'm coming. I've got a sister to rescue. Besides, it's a great plan. If we can get rid of Javeer and find Bron, it'll be worth all of my effort."

"Varak?" said Matt.

"You've both got guts, I'll give you that." Varak shook his head and chuckled. "Matt, I'm not convinced by everything you've said—and I'm not sure I believe your motives for being here, but it seems you're serious about getting rid of Javeer."

"Does that mean you'll help us?" asked Keir.

"Count me in. I want to get rid of Javeer more than you can imagine," said Varak. "And who knows . . . I might find my brother. Your crazy idea may just work."

Chapter 13

Varl could feel sweat running down his neck even though it had just been minutes since they'd exited the cage. He'd quickly grown accustomed to the dank smell and the dim lighting, but the oppressive heat was unbearable even with the enormous fans blasting air down the shafts. He found himself muttering, "deep, dark and hot," over and over again as he stumbled along behind Bronya and Sarven.

"Watch your footing here. The ground's *very* uneven," said Bronya, pointing to show him.

Varl looked down, and by the light on his helmet he saw that the rock floor suddenly dropped about three inches. "Thanks, my dear," he replied, glad that someone appreciated that he wasn't as agile as he used to be. He pressed his hand against the rock sidewall in an effort to maintain his balance as he stepped down, but he quickly drew it back. The wall was scorching! How stupid of him not to realize that at this depth the walls of the shafts would be hot to the touch.

The line came to a sudden halt.

"Stop here. Get into groups of three and collect your equipment," shouted one of the Gulden Guards as he walked the length of the line. "Three groups will stay and work at this level. The remaining two will be directed further."

Looking over the heads into the darkness, Varl could see the occasional flicker of lights down the tunnel. He strained to hear what was being said at the front of the line, but all he heard was a strange loud noise.

"Sarven," Varl called. "What's that noise?"

"Air hammers, I think," he replied.

"Air hammers, of course. Heavy, noisy things that create lots of dust as they drill into rock. I hope they're giving us face masks and gloves," said Varl.

"It's water I want," said Bronya. She dabbed her swollen lip with the edge of her tunic.

"Is your mouth all right?" asked Varl.

"I'll be fine, thanks," replied Bronya. "It was worth it to see the expression on Javeer's face. I'm just so thirsty. This heat is unbearable."

They reached a brightly lit, wide section of the tunnel where two guards passed out equipment. Another guard stood watch, his ST29 pointed at the line of workers.

Varl stepped up to the makeshift desk and willingly took a pair of leather gloves. "No mask?" he asked. The guard snorted and thrust an air hammer and a large metal bucket at him. "I guess not," said Varl, turning away from the desk.

He found himself facing a chain of huge hoppers, each one partially filled with rock. A locomotive attached to the front obviously pulled the load to the pithead.

"All those have got to be full before the end of this shift," snarled the guard. He pushed Varl forward, thumping him in the back with the butt of his ST29. "So stop looking at it and get to work."

"Which way?" asked Varl, staring at a fork in the tunnel.

"Your group went left," snapped the guard.

Varl began his journey down the next stretch of the shaft. Keeping up with Bronya and Sarven was more difficult than before. Not only was he now carrying a heavy air hammer and a bucket, but also the tunnel was less than five feet high and he had to bend over while he walked so as not to bump his head on the hangingwall.

The noise of air hammers was overpowering, which probably meant that he was approaching the rock face. Varl could see the pencil-thin stratum of gold in the sidewalls. He stopped to squat briefly and straighten his back, wondering how he would survive a whole day in a crouched position.

On the wall was a small device, which he realized was some kind of meter for measuring the levels of methane gas in the mine. Varl glanced at the red needle and was relieved to see it was pointing to low levels. He knew that if the air in the mine wasn't circulated properly, methane gas could build up and cause a massive explosion. He had heard mining stories of whole tunnels exploding inwards—footwall, hangingwall, sidewall, the lot—crushing everything in its way. Mining was such a dangerous business, he thought, although he was certain that Javeer hadn't installed the meters out of concern for his workers. Time was money, and an explosion could close Javeer's mining operation for days.

A billowing cloud of dust suddenly filled the tunnel. Varl quickly covered his nose and mouth, but not fast enough. He coughed and spluttered. This was unbearable, and he hadn't even begun! How was he going to work in these conditions without a mask? He sighed with relief when the haze cleared and he could make out the profiles of several people from his bunkhouse. Finally he had reached his destination. But where were Bronya and Sarven?

"Only three people are allowed at a work station," said a guard. "There's three already here so go on down to the bottom."

"This isn't the bottom?" Varl questioned.

The guard shook his head and pointed his ST29 toward a lower tunnel, which veered off to the right.

Varl trudged on, his clothing so wet with perspiration that it stuck to every part of his body. Now he knew why mines were often called the devil's workplace.

He staggered for another five minutes and finally saw his friends. "Bronya, Sarven, you're here," he gasped, near to collapse.

"You okay, old man?" asked Sarven.

"I will be when I've sat down for a moment," said Varl. "At least there are no guards watching over us."

"Very few guards will go as far as the equipment area because of the Gnashers," said Sarven. "So we'll rarely see one this far down. I bet that Horando has to pay them double."

Varl smiled. Gnashers! He hadn't seen any sign of such a thing.

"You needn't smile. I know what you're thinking, old man," said Sarven, his voice quaking. He looked nervously over his shoulder as though he expected something to suddenly fly out from the tunnel walls. "You just wait. You won't be smiling for long."

"Anyway," said Bronya, "we've got to get to work. Each group is expected to send up six buckets of rock per hour per group."

"Six? How do you know that?" asked Varl.

"One of the men in the line told me that."

"That's a total of forty-eight buckets between the three of us this shift!" exclaimed Sarven. "We'll never manage that."

"He also warned me that they make you work a double shift if you don't get all forty-eight."

Varl sighed. "Then I guess we'd better get to work. Don't think I could stand doing a double shift."

"How do we get the buckets to the surface?" asked Sarven.

"I think we carry them to the hoppers we saw," said Bronya.

Sarven sighed long and hard. "Right. I was afraid you'd say that." He turned on his air hammer. "It's going to be a long day."

Varl struggled to his feet and looked for the thin line of gold in the rock wall. Two buckets was a lot to fill and carry back up to the hoppers every hour. With his arthritis he had hardly managed the walk down here, and that was without carrying any rock. The youngsters were at a disadvantage by having him in their group—and for that he was very sorry.

* * * * *

Matt followed Varak and Keir down the dark tunnel that led from Mrs. Morsova's secret basement to the East End of Javeer. She had given them three old flashlights once used by the Underground and an assortment of heavy tools. Even though they had left her cottage over an hour ago, Matt could still taste her delicious rabbit stew on his tongue. He'd savored every mouthful, knowing it might be his last meal for a while.

Matt stepped out to catch up with Varak, who'd set a fast pace. Varak had an old map, which showed two entrances on the north side of Mount Boro-Boro that Javeer had closed when he took over the mine. Varak had stumbled on one entrance by chance a year ago. According to the map, it connected with the main shaft and that was to be their destination.

Timing would be crucial. Varak had told them that the night shift had fewer workers and fewer Gulden Guards on duty than the other two shifts. So night would be their best chance to get into the new tunnels without being seen. They were aiming to be in the mine before dark and into Javeer's tunnels by three in the morning.

"How much longer?" asked Matt, pausing for a

moment to catch his breath.

Varak stopped and waited for Matt and Keir to catch up. "Only another couple of minutes to the end of the tunnel. We're walking under the northern corner of the East End of Javeer right now. The tunnel will bring us up into fields on the outskirts of the city. Then it'll take another hour around to the north side of the mountain."

"That's okay," said Keir. "We'll make it before dark."

"At this pace? No problem!" quipped Matt. He rubbed his arms to warm them up. It was definitely getting cooler as the tunnel went deeper underground.

Varak started walking again, but more slowly. "We'll be out in the open for about ten minutes after we leave the tunnel. We know the Gulden Guards are looking for us, so we'll have to be really careful."

"No kidding," said Keir. "Matt's attracted Javeer's curiosity and my sister has defied him. He won't stop until he's caught us all."

"Can't believe that Gorbun snitched on us again," growled Matt. "That scum bag."

Keir nodded. "It had to be him. No one else knew we were on a rescue mission."

"Good job we fed him false information," said Matt.

"Well, we've definitely got Javeer worried," laughed Keir. "He's probably trying to work out how a stranger with a computer is going to get through his main gates!"

"With any luck he'll continue to believe that," said Varak. "He won't be expecting what we've got planned for him. The Underground has never tried to sabotage his prisons or his gold mine because everyone is too terrified of ST29s. We've never had any weapons to defend ourselves. Javeer won't anticipate a little creativity on our part."

Matt had regained his breath by the time they stopped at the base of a rickety wooden ladder. He looked up and gasped. "You've got to be joking!" he said, rattling the bottom. "This thing isn't safe and it's at least thirty feet tall!"

"Forty feet, actually. And it's okay, *really*. I climb *this thing* several times a month," said Varak. "It shakes a little where a few bolts have come loose, but it will hold our weight."

"We're going up one at a time, right?" said Keir, tugging at the bottom. "Don't think it will take the weight of three of us."

Varak pulled a face. "I'm not that stupid," he replied. "Okay. The tunnel comes out in the corner of a farmer's field. The entrance is hidden by a clump of tree stumps. There's not usually anyone walking down the road nearby—but check to be sure. When you climb out, lie flat on the ground. Just watch out for the bull."

Matt choked. "Did you say a bull?"

Varak laughed. "Don't worry—he's pretty old. He won't bother you, but he does keep the Gulden Guards from entering the field and discovering the tunnel."

"So who's first?" asked Keir.

"Me," said Matt, eager to get it over and done with. He hated heights. Although he'd climbed higher than this before in Zaul, the added anxiety that the ladder might collapse on him was a little more than he could bear.

Taking a deep breath, he grabbed the rungs and placed his foot on the bottom bar. The ladder seemed okay, so he began the climb—slowly at first, then more quickly as his confidence grew. The wood creaked and groaned with every movement. After a while he took a rest and looked down at Keir and Varak, dwarfed by the height. Big mistake. The height was dizzying. His palms grew sweaty and slipped on the bars. He gulped and continued slowly upwards.

How much farther? He looked up. Second big mistake. He had as far to climb as he'd already come. This ladder was never ending! His heart beat furiously and his ears buzzed. *Come on*, he told himself. *You've done worse before. Just don't look down.*

"You're almost there!" Varak shouted from below.

The words were encouraging. Matt continued, counting every rung as he went and concentrating on the opening at the top. Yes, he was definitely beginning to conquer his fear of heights, but now he was worried about the bull.

Finally he reached the top, stuck his head out into the open, and took a quick look around the snowy field. The bull stood in the far corner and there was no sign of anyone passing by on the nearby road. Matt hauled himself onto the grass. He quickly buttoned up his jacket—it was much colder outside with the howling icy wind than it had been in the tunnel. He lay in the snow, shivering and getting wetter by the minute. Perhaps going first had not been the right decision. Thank goodness that Keir had given him a change of clothing to put in his pack. He positioned himself between two tree stumps where the snow hadn't collected as much.

Within minutes Keir joined him, shortly followed by Varak, who seemed to arrive in half the time.

"You guys okay?" asked Varak.

"Cold and wet, but we'll survive," said Matt.

"Okay. Let's go. No sense in lying here freezing any longer than we have to," said Varak.

They skulked across the field to the road and then through the fields beyond. As usual, Matt was scrambling to keep up with Varak's fast pace. The craggy snow-covered mountain loomed in front of them, a pretty picture against the deep blue sky. Matt reflected on all that he had been through in the past few days. Targon weighed heavily on his mind. Where was he? And was Varl okay?

Matt couldn't wait to get into the mine and begin the next part of his journey. He knew that Level 4 of his game was reaching its climax and he was desperate to rescue Varl, but he had nagging doubts about what awaited them. Would the Gnashers really help, or were they to be feared as everyone had warned?

Before he started down the mine he'd look at the rhyme again. He had to be sure that he wasn't missing a vital clue.

Chapter 14

Varl's heart leaped into his mouth when he heard the deafening sound of a blaring horn. He turned off his air hammer and stared at Bronya and Sarven. "Does that mean what I think it means?"

Sarven nodded. "Uh-huh. End of the shift."

"By my reckoning we're six buckets short of our forty-eight," said Bronya, her face showing a mixture of disappointment and exhaustion.

Varl sat slowly down on the dusty uneven ground. "That's what I'd figured too. I'm afraid an old man like me isn't much good at a task like this. I'm sorry that I've let you both down."

"Nonsense!" said Sarven. "We wouldn't have anyone else with us, would we, Bronya?"

Bronya draped her arm around Varl's shoulders. "We certainly wouldn't! Besides, I think that Sarven here did most of the work. I don't think I carried many more buckets than you."

Varl smiled. "You're too nice, both of you. I guess this means we're down here for another eight hours."

"Well, we'll make our way back with everyone else, and who knows, we might just get overlooked by the guards," said Sarven.

Varl dragged himself to his feet, massaged the small of his back, put on the green backpack and then picked up his tools. His chest felt tight with dust, and he coughed violently as he followed Sarven and Bronya up the winding tunnels.

He arrived at the tool supply desk just as Sarven was laying his air hammer down on the rough wooden countertop. Several guards had congregated to take equipment off the prisoners. Varl counted three guards at the desk and two more by the hoppers. All five of them were huge and muscular, and all five were armed with ST29s.

"What's this?" one of the guards snapped, his face contorted into an irate expression.

"My equipment," said Sarven. "We hand it back to you at the end of the shift, right?"

The guard walked from behind the desk and thrust the air hammer hard at Sarven. "You three aren't done for the day," he barked. "You've another six buckets to fetch, and only then will you be allowed back to the bunkhouse. Now get going!"

Varl groaned and staggered back down the tunnel. At least they didn't have to do a complete second shift, just finish up the forty-eight bucket quota. "Hopefully we'll be done in another couple of hours," he said to Bronya. "That's not so bad, right?"

She smiled weakly at him. "It could have been much worse, I suppose. I'm just so tired and hot right now that another six buckets seems like the world."

"Let's get a system going here," said Sarven, sounding energetic. "I'm the strongest. I can probably carry two buckets at a time. You and Bronya can mine the rock and I'll do the carrying."

"You'll be exhausted!" said Bronya.

"Nope. I'll be fine. Let's try it, at least."

"Okay," said Varl. "We'll try it for an hour and see what progress we make." He knew that Sarven was trying to keep Bronya going. He admired the boy's courage.

* * * * *

"Great going, Jake! We've found the rear entrance," said Targon, looking at the old mine shaft on the screen. It was partially hidden by tall grass and rocks, but there it was. "Now we just have to figure out what to do next. Pull up the third rhyme again, will you?"

"Sure. There you go." Jake clicked on the mouse. "Don't ask me what we should do. If we don't have weapons, I don't have a clue."

Targon reread the rhyme, sounding out the words carefully. He was getting better at reading, he decided. He just needed a bit more time.

"Not bad," said Jake when he had finished. "You're getting better. Won't be long before you read as fast as me."

"Thanks," said Targon, knowing that was a rare compliment from Jake. "Well, it says to use technology not weapons to prepare. But what technology have we got?"

Jake tipped the computer chair back so far that he almost lay flat. He seemed to be staring at the ceiling, as if the white speckled surface would give him a good idea.

"We have the mining equipment," he suddenly said. "That's the technology we have. There's the winding gear that takes the workers down in the cage and the locomotives that bring up the hoppers full of rock."

"Hmm," said Targon. "I guess we could stop the locomotives from working so that they can't bring stuff up."

Jake groaned. "No, that won't shut the mine down. Javeer will just get the locomotives fixed."

"Hmm. This is a tough one," said Targon.

"And then of course there are the huge fans that keep the mine cool and get rid of the toxic gases," said Jake.

"Toxic gases?" asked Targon.

"Yeah. Too much methane gas and . . . Kaboom! The whole mine'll blow up! Now *that* could shut down a mine for years!"

"Yes! That's our answer!" said Targon, feeling suddenly optimistic. "That's how we'll shut down the mine."

"But of course you'd have to get all the workers out first," said Jake. "You did tell me that the object of this Keeper game is to free the people—not kill 'em all off, right?" He laughed loudly, his silver braces glinting under the ceiling lights.

Targon laughed with him, but his mind was in a whirl. Jake had come up with an excellent solution, but they couldn't risk setting off any kind of explosion without first being sure that everyone was out of the mine. "That's going to be difficult. Any suggestions?"

"I'm trying to remember what I learned about mines," said Jake, finally tipping his chair forward again. He began to swivel round and round. "They have methane gas measuring equipment in the shafts. I guess we could stop the fans from working long enough to get the gas levels to rise in the shafts." He paused and thought for a moment. "But then we'd have to fix the gas meters so they'd read extreme levels of methane. That would make the guards clear everyone out quickly . . . or something like that."

"Jake, this is great! I'm sure we're on to something here!" said Targon, hardly able to contain his excitement. "How do you reckon we can do this?"

"Well, what about these Gnasher things?"

"I'd forgotten about them," said Targon.

"We're supposed to work *with* them, right?"

"That's what it says."

"Well, the rhyme is actually pretty ambiguous," said Jake.

"Ambiguous?"

"Yeah, it's not very clear. It could mean a couple of things. It could mean that we use technology when we prepare to get rid of Horando Javeer, or it could also mean we use technology when we prepare to work with the Gnashers. Or it could mean both, I suppose."

"But how can you use technology to work with creatures or monsters or whatever those Gnasher things are?" asked Targon. "Do they talk or something? Pull up the menu, and let's see what else is on the list."

"Well, we've covered *Maps, Transportation, Underground, Weapons, Food, Supplies* and *Keeper*," said Jake, pointing at each menu item. "I guess that leaves Number 8, *'Help,'* I think we could do with some of that right now."

"Okay, click on that and see what it says."

Suddenly the screen was filled with flying golden spheres, about the size of baseballs, with translucent green wings. They zoomed in every direction.

"Whoa! Look at that!" screamed Targon, ducking instinctively as another sphere zoomed toward them. "Did you see the teeth on that thing? They're like hundreds of tiny white pointed spikes! What *are* those things?"

"They're Gnashers, I guess," said Jake.

"I know that!" Targon shot back. "I mean, *what* are they? Are they alive or are they androids or what?"

"Androids?" Jake shook his head. "Nah. They look like life forms to me. They've got light green wings and teeth, don't they?" said Jake, staring at the screen.

"But they don't have eyes," said Targon. "Their bodies shine like they're made of metal and they don't seem to be making any noise. What makes something alive?"

Jake shrugged. "I flunked Biology. But I think that humans and animals are all carbon-based creatures."

"Click on the information box. What does it say about them?" Targon suggested.

Jake moved the mouse and clicked. A box flashed up at the bottom of the screen. He cleared his throat. "It says: *Gnashers are silicon-based life forms. They can communicate with humans by transmitting information through wireless signals that can be read as pictures."*

"Transmitting pictures? That's different!"

"But there's your answer," said Jake. "They're silicon-based life forms, not carbon-based."

"Which means?"

Jake turned to Targon and flashed a big silver smile. "They eat rock."

* * * * *

"I see the entrance!" shouted Varak. He scrambled up the side of the mountain, slipping on the scree and digging his shovel in as leverage. "Come on, you two!"

Matt grabbed the stalks of the tall grasses so that he wouldn't slip back, and clambered up to where Varak was waiting. Keir was only seconds behind.

"Told you I'd find it again without any trouble," Varak said. He motioned to the huge pile of rocks blocking the entrance. "'Course it'll take some time to clear this lot away, even with three of us."

"There's an opening near the top but I don't think we'll get through," said Matt.

"No," Varak replied. "We'll have to clear more rock away from around it."

"Another hour and it'll be dark. We can't do much with only a couple of flashlights and we'll need to save the batteries for inside the mine," said Keir.

"Well, we can make a start. We'll find some shelter

amongst the boulders when it gets too dark to see," said Varak.

Matt opened his backpack. "I've got to get out of these wet things before I do anything else." He pulled out a pair of pants, dark green sweater and worn socks that Keir had lent him, shivering in the icy wind as he changed clothes. His denim jacket was soaked through, but at least he wouldn't need it in the mine.

Varak and Keir had removed only a few of the fallen rocks from the entrance by the time he'd changed. This was going to be a long job. He decided to take a few minutes to open up his laptop and read the rhyme one last time. He perched himself on top of a flat boulder with a large overhang on one side. The surface had been worn smooth by the wind over the years.

He opened up his game, scrolled down the menu and clicked on Number 7, 'Weapons.' The rhyme appeared in white cursive lettering on a dark background.

"Know the Gnashers if you dare, use technology not weapons to prepare," Matt read quietly. "With their Keeper fight a common foe . . ." Yes, the rhyme was definitely telling him to work with the Keeper of the Gnashers. But how? In Boro everyone he'd met was terrified of the Gnashers. What were these things and how could he contact them? How would he find their Keeper? More important, how could he prevent the Gnashers from attacking once they entered the mine?

Suddenly Matt's screen went blank. "Oh, just great! Don't pack up on me now!" This could really mean trouble.

The battery must be dead. But that wasn't possible. He'd hardly used his laptop on this level.

"What's the problem?" asked Keir, removing a rock from the pile. He walked over to where Matt was sitting and climbed up onto the boulder next to him.

"Not sure," said Matt, hammering on the *'Enter'* key. "I thought I'd better check the rhyme one more time, but I've never had this happen before. The screen's gone completely blank, but the battery level is okay. Whoa . . . what's happening now?"

"There are fuzzy lines all over the screen," said Keir.

"What does that mean?"

Varak joined them, leaning over the top of the boulder. "What's up?"

Matt shook his head. "Never seen anything like this before. It's like static on the screen. The computer seems to have frozen. I can't pull up any information, I can't shut the thing down and I've got weird wavy lines and dots flashing at me."

"So what are you going to do?" asked Varak.

Matt's stomach was churning. What could he do out here in the middle of nowhere? He'd checked all the obvious things. If he couldn't access his game information he was stuck in Boro, and Varl and Targon would be in real trouble. For someone who thought he knew so much about computers, he suddenly felt inadequate.

"Oh no! Gnashers! They're coming out of the tunnel," screamed Keir. "Get down!"

Matt looked up from his computer in time to see at

least a hundred golden spheres zooming from the small hole in the side of the mountain, heading straight for him. They were mesmerizing.

Varak tugged at Matt's pants. "Matt, get off there, now! Get under this overhang!"

Matt stared upwards at the golden spheres, their green wings glinting against the icy early evening sky. They began to circle him in swirling patterns.

"Matt! They'll kill you!" Varak shouted again.

"No, it's okay," said Matt. He felt surprisingly calm holding onto his computer.

"Matt! Have you lost your mind? Get down here," Keir begged. "They'll eat you alive!"

But Matt stayed glued to his spot, entranced by the gleaming bodies and their movement around him. Keir and Varak's voices seemed to fade into oblivion.

"Matt! Matt! Get under here with us!"

Was that Keir's voice?

The Gnashers encircled him, but stayed at least six feet away. Evenly spaced, they swirled in waves above his head. It was as if he were looking at a swarm of large bees. Their wings fluttered in a blur and they emitted a strange high-pitched buzzing sound. And even though he could clearly see their jagged rows of teeth, he didn't feel threatened.

Matt's computer began to vibrate in his hands. When he looked down at the screen, a series of video clips flashed before him over and over again. There were pictures of the Gnashers, pictures of the tunnels in the mines, and pictures of the dead Gulden Guards. His head pounded. What *was* this?

One of the Gnashers dived straight for the computer. Matt instinctively wrapped his arms around his most prized possession. But instead of attacking Matt or his laptop, the Gnasher hovered above the screen for a few seconds and then flew in an intricate pattern between Matt and the laptop. It then returned to circle above with the others.

Then Matt understood. The Gnashers were trying to communicate with him through his computer.

"Keir, Varak, take a look at this. The Gnashers are using my computer to talk to us!"

"Yeah, right." Keir laughed nervously from under the overhang.

"I'm serious!" shouted Matt. "Get up here, both of you. Take a look at these pictures."

Keir slowly got off the ground. With his head scrunched down into his shoulders as if he were trying to protect his neck, he looked first at the Gnashers above and then raised himself to full height. He stared at the screen and then into the air. "Are you sure *they're* sending those pictures?"

"No question," said Matt.

"How *can* you be sure?"

"Call it gut instinct. Plus, my computer was frozen up, remember? I've no control over it at the moment. I guess they're somehow sending signals that are being picked up by the wireless Ethernet on my computer."

"They don't *seem* like they're going to attack us," said

Varak, finally emerging from the safety of the rock overhang. He glanced above and then slowly rose to his feet. "I wish they'd back away a bit. All those teeth are terrifying."

"You'll be okay," said Matt with confidence. "They would've attacked us long ago if they were going to."

Keir shuddered. "I hope you're right," he said, protectively pulling up his collar around his neck. "What do you think they're trying to tell us?"

"Well, if you look at these pictures of the mine shafts you can see the Gnashers," said Matt. "But if you look closely, they seem to disappear when they hit the sides of the tunnels."

"No, I don't think that's what is happening," said Varak. He pointed to the bottom of the screen. "Look closely here and here. It sounds weird, but it looks to me like the Gnashers are somehow pushing through the rock, making new tunnels as they go."

Matt grinned. Now things were beginning to make sense. "No, it's not weird. I'll bet you anything they're silicon-based life forms."

"Silicon what?" said Keir, looking up at the Gnashers again.

"Silicon-based life forms," repeated Matt. "Life forms that survive by extracting the minerals from the rocks. I didn't really believe it was possible. Basically, they eat mineral-rich rock—you know, the kind of rock that has gold in it."

Keir gave him a quizzical look.

"Just look at those pictures of dead Gulden Guards," Varak said. "Pretty gruesome. It makes me very uncomfortable to see pictures like that with the killer creatures circling above." He shuddered noticeably.

"I know. They keep flashing that clip at me," said Matt. "That's about the tenth time I've seen it and I still don't know what to make of it. I keep thinking about the rhyme. It said that we're to work with their Keeper to fight a common foe. Which one is their Keeper, do you think?"

Keir looked up and shrugged. "They all look the same to me."

"And who's our common foe?" questioned Matt.

"Well, that's easy. It has to be Horando Javeer and his Gulden Guards," said Varak. "If the Gnashers live in the mines and survive on the rock, as you are suggesting, they can't be happy about Horando Javeer and his mining. Javeer is probably taking away all the minerals they need to survive, forcing them to go deeper and deeper below ground."

"That's it!" said Keir. "Why did I never think of this before? All the dead bodies we've ever seen from Gnasher attacks have been Gulden Guards. I've never heard of a civilian being killed by a Gnasher."

"I think you're right," said Varak. "Javeer sent prisoners down into the mines because so many Guards were being attacked that they refused to work in the deeper tunnels. And even though civilians are now doing the mining I've still only heard about Gulden Guards who've been killed by the Gnashers."

"So why didn't Gnashers attack citizens of Boro when they were mining twenty years ago, before Javeer arrived?" asked Matt.

"The mining was very limited. Gold was extracted only as it was needed, and never at the depths that Javeer has now tunneled. Javeer is taking huge amounts of gold. At this rate there'll be nothing left in a few years."

"Which means that the Gnashers would have nothing left either," said Matt. "The survival of their species depends on the gold."

Keir sighed. "Pity I didn't think about all this before, and more of a pity that the Underground didn't figure it out before! It would have been to our advantage."

"You didn't think about it before because everyone's so terrified of Javeer and his men that you focused on getting rid of him and keeping citizens of Boro out of the mines," said Matt.

"The Gnashers are backing off," said Varak, relief evident in his voice.

Matt looked up to see the swarm of shining spheres hovering at the partially cleared entrance to the mine. Suddenly there was an ear-piercing metallic screech, and tiny particles of rock spewed everywhere as a huge cloud of dust billowed upwards.

"I don't believe it," said Varak, moving closer to the entrance. "They do eat rock. They're clearing the rest of the entrance for us."

"Well, I never thought I'd say this, but I guess your rhyme was right after all," said Keir, shaking his head in disbelief. "We're actually going to be working with the Gnashers. Unbelievable!"

Matt closed his laptop. "Well, the Gnashers will be very useful if we come across a blocked tunnel. No shovels and no digging. I'm all for that."

"I suggest that we still bring *all* the shovels," said Varak in an authoritative tone. "We don't know what lies ahead or what the Gnashers will do for us, if anything."

Matt jumped down from the boulder and slung his pack on his back. "So what are we waiting for? It's dark and I'm cold standing out here. Let's get going!"

Chapter 15

Yarl groaned as he lowered himself onto his bed. Bronya was already asleep and Sarven snored above him. It had been one very long day. His back ached, his legs ached, his arms ached. In fact, he couldn't name one part of his body that didn't hurt. Thank goodness it had only taken two hours to make up the remaining buckets for the shift. At least they had arrived back at the bunkhouse in time to get food, if you could call it that. His stomach growled with hunger. Lunch had been a dried-up piece of bread and a tiny morsel of meat, and their evening meal some kind of disgusting vegetable slop.

He felt depressed. In this state, how could he possibly help Matt? Last night his spirits had been high as he'd thought about scouting out the gold mine in preparation for Matt and the Underground. And now, tonight, he wasn't fit for anything. He wondered how he could possibly work this hard again tomorrow and the next day . . . and more days after that.

And yet, even though he was physically exhausted, his mind was so restless that he couldn't sleep. He tried to remember every step of their journey into the mine, and began counting the guards he'd passed en route to the bottom of the pit. He thought about how many workers could fit into the cage at one time, and the equipment they'd been given to extract the rock. Surely with all that equipment and the high number of prisoners at HJG he could organize some kind of rebellion.

He sighed. Who was he kidding? The guards were armed with ST29s, and often whips as well, and the workers were not only too terrified to rebel but also too exhausted. Tired and malnourished workers carrying only air hammers and shovels were no match for even a few heavily armed guards. He had to come up with a creative escape plan that relied on no one but himself to see it through.

"Use your brains, Varl!" he muttered. "It's what you're good at! And it's all you have now that your body is old."

He rolled onto his left side and began to picture the mine and the locomotives that carried the rock to the surface. He thought about the huge winding gear, the fans that vented the shafts, and the methane gas detectors on the walls.

"Wait a minute . . . methane gas!" Varl sat up quickly in his bunk, nearly hitting his head on Sarven's bed above. "Methane gas!" How much could the gas build up in the shaft before everyone had to be evacuated? In fact, how much methane would it take to cause an explosion?

Varl's heart was racing and once again excitement flowed through him. Tomorrow he'd take a look at a methane gas meter, but he'd need something to pry off the cover. "I know what I need," he muttered.

Varl quietly got out of bed and lifted his mattress. He had noticed when making his bed that several of the springs underneath were broken, and the thin pieces of metal that connected them hung loose. Patiently he wiggled one of the pieces back and forth until it broke free. He put it under his pillow, knowing that it might make all the difference the next day. He'd just have to find a way to conceal it in his clothing.

He smiled to himself. Perhaps an old man with an aging body could still be a worthy opponent.

* * * * *

Matt followed Varak down the shaft, Keir on his heels. After only thirty minutes he was already wet with perspiration. The sweater he'd been so grateful for outside now seemed about to smother him. He put out his hand against the sidewall to steady himself. "Wow! Even the walls are warm."

"It's going to get much worse than this as we go deeper," said Varak. "You'll hardly be able to touch the walls in a while. I've been told that even with huge fans venting the new shafts, at the bottom of the pit the heat is almost unbearable. You'd better pray that the old and new shafts connect. Otherwise it may get too hot in this old shaft for us to continue."

"We'll do it. We've got to," said Matt, trying to stay optimistic. The heat was one thing he hadn't considered.

The Gnashers had entered the shaft before them but

soon disappeared into the blackness beyond. He had no idea where they'd gone, but Matt had a feeling he'd be seeing them again before too long.

With the fear of the Gnashers diminished, Matt had seen a change in both Keir and Varak. Both were more confident and certainly more eager to get into the mine and get the job done. Varak's enthusiasm showed in his fast pace, and Keir's in his non-stop talking about what he'd do to Horando Javeer should he meet him face to face.

"Stop a minute, will you?" said Matt, placing his flashlight at his feet. "Sorry, but I've got to take off this sweater."

Varak halted. "Now that you mention it, I'd do better without mine as well."

Keir stripped off his shirt and stuffed it into his pack. "Drink, anyone?" he asked as he took out a canteen of water.

Matt took just a tiny sip, painfully aware that once their supply was gone there wouldn't be any more. "Are we on track?" he asked.

Varak unfolded the map. "Well, we passed that fork to the left and the tunnel has definitely narrowed like it shows here," he said, tapping the map's centerfold. "And according to this height marker, the roof, or hangingwall as they call it in a mine, drops by at least two feet. I think we'll be crawling soon."

"How far do you reckon we still have to go before we join up with Javeer's new shafts?" asked Keir.

Varak pointed to the map again. "The Underground intelligence network estimates that Javeer has mined to about here. I would guess we've still got several hours of walking or crawling."

"Once we get there we'll need the workers to help us clear the mine before we destroy it," Keir warned. "Otherwise we won't know how many shafts are open, and how many people are down there."

Matt sighed. Every level in his computer game got harder and this one suddenly seemed impossible. "Let's hope we can find Varl and Bronya. They'll be our best bet. Varl's got a wealth of information, and they can be trusted."

"Agreed, but first things first," said Varak. "Let's concentrate on connecting with Javeer's shafts and then we'll worry about shutting down the mine. Okay, everyone ready?"

Varak set off at a fast pace once again and Matt could feel sweat from his drenched hair dripping onto his shoulders. The heat was already oppressive. How would they survive the journey in this stifling air? He was glad when the roof of the tunnel lowered and they had to slow down and walk stooped over.

And then they came to a full stop.

Varak threw his backpack to the ground and sighed. "I knew things were going too well."

The tunnel was blocked with debris. Judging by the settled pile of rocks, Matt guessed the tunnel had caved in several years before.

"Now what?" asked Keir.

"Well, the Gnashers are nowhere in sight, so I guess we have to dig our way through," he said.

"But what do we do with the rock we're removing?" asked Keir. "We don't want to block the tunnel behind us in case we need to come back this way."

Varak turned to look at the shaft behind them. "Trouble is, it's a long way back to that fork in the tunnel. It'll take us forever to carry rocks that far."

"But there's nowhere else to put them," said Matt. "We'll just have to do the best we can and stack the rocks along the sides. Hopefully we can still leave enough room to get through."

Suddenly out of the darkness came at least a dozen winged golden spheres, glinting in the beam from Matt's flashlight. "The Gnashers are back!" he said excitedly. "They're here to help us."

"Said with such certainty," said Varak, ducking as one Gnasher after another flew between him and the sidewall of the shaft. "Not sure I'm quite as trusting as you. Half of me wants to run as fast as I can in the other direction."

"I know what you mean," said Keir. "Images of dead bodies covered in teeth marks are still fresh in my mind. But I *think* I'm glad to see them."

The Gnashers hovered over the pile of fallen rocks. They dodged around each other, up and down, side to side. Matt tried to follow them with his eyes but their flitting made him dizzy.

"This is different," he said. "They didn't do this before.

They flew in slow circling patterns and in formation."

"Do you think there's a problem?" asked Keir. "Hope they're not going to suddenly turn on us."

Matt shook his head. "They'd have killed us the moment we entered the mine if they were going to."

"Maybe it's too much rock for them to eat their way through," suggested Varak.

"Nah," said Matt. "We saw what they did to the rocks at the entrance in just a few minutes, and that was way worse than this. No, it's like they're trying to tell us something."

"Perhaps they want us to move back in the shaft," said Varak. "We'll get covered in rock dust if we stand here."

"I'll bet that's it," said Matt, immediately walking at least ten yards back down the shaft, with Varak and Keir following behind. This time he was prepared for the fountain of dust and the ear-shattering noise. He shone his flashlight ahead at the wall of rock and watched as the Gnashers tunneled easily through the debris. Before too long they had created a perfectly round hole right through the center.

"Yes!" Matt cheered. "I knew they'd help us." He watched the Gnashers zoom past them and disappear once again into the blackness. "Thank you," he called out, feeling he had to say it but not expecting them to understand his words. He walked toward the newly formed tunnel. They would have to crawl through, but at least the hole was big enough even with packs on their backs.

"What do you think?" asked Varak. "Is it safe?"

"I can't see how long it is," said Matt, shining his flashlight through the opening. "One of us should try it first in case we have to back up."

"Good idea," said Varak. "Any volunteers?"

Matt laughed. "I'll go. I've got faith in our spherical friends."

He found his footing on the bottom rocks and climbed into the tunnel. It was big enough that he could crawl on his hands and knees. "It's looking good," he called back.

Before long he reached the other end, and saw the open mineshaft before him. "All clear," he called back. "It's not very far."

Varak and Keir each crawled though the tunnel and were soon standing beside him. Matt looked at his watch under the beam. "It's ten o'clock already. We ought to get a few hours' sleep before we go any farther."

"I agree," said Varak. "We won't be able to sleep at all if it gets any hotter."

Matt positioned his pack as a pillow, and lay down in the shaft on the sweater that Keir had given him. He was so tired from such an eventful and strenuous few days that he hardly noticed how uncomfortable the ground was. He closed his eyes. Images of Varl and Targon flashed through his mind. "Tomorrow," he muttered. "Tomorrow I'll find you both."

Chapter 16

Varl leaped from his bed at the sound of the morning whistle, feeling rejuvenated. It was amazing what a good night's sleep and the beginnings of an escape plan had done for his spirits. Today he'd take action. He felt under his pillow for the thin piece of wire and poked it into the hem of his tunic.

"Get up, Bronya. Sarven, wake up!" he said, shaking Sarven's legs. "We haven't long before we're back in the mine, so you've got to eat."

Bronya stretched her arms above her head and got up. She smiled at Varl and muttered, "Morning." Varl saw her mouth was no longer swollen, but a bruised area still showed on her lower lip.

Sarven dragged himself off the top bunk and threw on his clean clothing in a dazed stupor. He winced as he pulled his arms through his shirt-sleeves. "My arms and shoulders are aching before I even start," he grumbled.

Varl wasn't surprised. Yesterday had been a tough day for the boy. Sarven had done most of the heavy work to make up for Varl's inability. Today would be even harder if Sarven were sore before he started.

"Got something to tell you both," said Varl as they sat down to eat.

Sarven shoveled in a spoonful of stodge and grimaced as he swallowed. "What's that, old man?"

"I've got the beginnings of a plan to get us out of here," said Varl enthusiastically, in an effort to get them excited.

"Yeah, right," said Sarven, pushing his bowl away after only a couple of spoonfuls. "The beginnings . . . I know what that means."

Bronya pulled a half-hearted smile. "Let us know when you've got it all figured out."

"I really do need your help in this," said Varl, talking in a hushed tone and trying to adopt a more serious mood. He pushed Sarven's bowl back in front of him. "So eat up because you'll need your strength. Remember the methane gas monitors on the sidewalls in the mine?"

"Uh-huh," said Sarven. He lifted his bowl close to his mouth and shoveled in another spoonful, eyeing Varl over the top of the bowl. "What about them?"

"I need to get close to one to take a really good look. There was one by the desk where we got our air hammers, but there were too many guards there. There was also one that we passed on the level above where we were working. I could see only one Gulden Guard close by—so that's my best bet."

"Okay," said Sarven, showing a little more interest. "So what do you want us to do?"

"Distract the guard," said Varl.

"Yeah, right," said Sarven. "Just like that."

"I'm sure that one of you can think of something," said

Varl. He leaned across the table and lowered his voice to a whisper. "The buildup of methane gas in a mine can cause a huge explosion. But Javeer won't take that risk because his mining operations would close permanently. I know that the explosive range is between 5% and 15% methane-in-air. So all I have to do is change the settings on the gas meters so the gas levels appear to be dangerously close to the explosive range. We could get the mine shut down for a few days."

"Well that would give us a rest, but it won't get rid of Javeer," said Bronya.

"Agreed," said Varl. "But it would mean we could get all the workers out of the mine long enough for us to get back in and destroy it. That way no one gets hurt."

"Okay, old man," said Sarven. "The first part of your plan seems reasonable and fairly easy. But you don't have a second part to the plan at all! Destroying the mine shafts will take explosives . . . which we don't have!"

"I didn't say this was going to be easy or quick," said Varl. "It'll take a while to work it out, but I know we'll find a way. So, are you both in on this today?"

Bronya nodded. "I'll do my best," she said.

"Uh-huh," said Sarven. "Of course."

The main door of bunkhouse 157 opened, bringing freezing air into the room. The mine guard stood in the open doorway and ordered them to line up.

Varl followed Bronya and Sarven, determined to find a way to make his plan work.

He passed the huge fans, slowing his pace to get a

look at how they were powered. Good news. Thick electric cables ran from the overhead power lines into the powerhouse. He knew a lot about electricity.

A smile crept across his lips. They didn't need explosives to destroy the mine! Everything he needed was staring him right in the face, and it was above ground and easily accessible. How he wished that Matt and Targon were here to share his excitement.

Varl squeezed into the cage, and as the door slid closed he turned to Sarven and whispered, "I just came up with the second part of the plan."

Sarven frowned. "Yeah, right," he mouthed back.

Varl sighed. It would take a lot to convince the boy.

The long walk through the tunnels seemed to go quickly. Varl was so pumped up with adrenaline that he didn't think about how hot he was or how many steps he was taking. His mind was elsewhere, plotting and scheming. Before long they were lining up to collect their buckets and air hammers. But this time Varl could hardly wait to start down the next section of the tunnel. He watched the Gulden Guards closely. They were standing in exactly the same positions as the day before.

"Hold back," he whispered to Bronya and Sarven as they started walking. "Let the group in front get a long way ahead of us."

Sarven slowed his pace as instructed. Varl shone his flashlight along the walls. Where was the methane gas meter? He was sure he had seen one in this area. Surely he hadn't missed it.

"There it is!" he whispered. "You two keep a lookout. Yesterday there was one guard standing just before the tunnels divided for the last time."

Bronya and Sarven walked a little farther and stopped just before a bend in the tunnel. They waved an all-clear signal at Varl.

He turned his attention back to the meter. Just as he had remembered, a square cover with a plastic window protected it. As far as he could see there were no screws holding it on and the cover was simply snapped in place.

He poked the hidden piece of wire back through his tunic hem and pushed it under the edge of the cover, attempting to pry it off. The first two corners snapped off easily but the last two stuck fast. *Easy does it*, he reminded himself. If he broke the cover it would be obvious that someone had tampered with the equipment.

Finally Varl heard that reassuring snap and the lid fell into his hand. He studied the wiring, and saw that rechargeable batteries powered the meter. Removing a battery would be too obvious and too easily fixed. He had to find something that wouldn't be detected.

"Okay, let's take a look," he muttered. "There's a simple on/off switch and there's a flashing indicator for when gas levels are too high. Hmm. Not difficult." He traced the wiring for the LCD display. Perhaps he could short-circuit the sensor so the display would read a higher gas concentration than there actually was. Could he do it with only that thin piece of metal?

Bronya ran back to Varl. "The guard's coming. We can

see a flashlight down the tunnel. How much longer do you need?"

"Three minutes should do it," said Varl. "Just keep him from looking at this wall."

"We'll walk down the tunnel to meet him," said Bronya. "Good luck."

Within seconds he could hear the drawling voice of the guard he'd met yesterday and Bronya's higher-pitched chatter. Time was running out and his arthritic fingers were causing him problems. How he wished that he were ten years younger and that his fingers would bend easily.

Varl stabbed the metal piece underneath the mélange of wires and onto the tiny terminals of the sensor. The numbers began to climb steadily. His plan was working. The red light started to flash as if the methane gas levels were dangerously high. Perfect! He jammed the bent piece of metal in position on the terminals, pushing it down under the wiring to hide it. That should do it. Now all he had to do was replace the cover.

"Why are you not with the rest of your party?" a deep voice bellowed nearby.

Varl turned just as the flashlight of the approaching guard hit him. He held the cover tightly behind his back, and leaned against the wall, making sure the meter was hidden. What could he do? Blood surged through his veins and his heart beat furiously. He wondered if guilt showed on his face, and prayed that if the guard saw his flushed face in the dim light, he'd assume it was from the effects of the heat.

"I didn't feel well and had to rest," said Varl in a weak voice. He panted heavily for added effect. "I'll be fine in a while."

"You've got one minute to join those two kids or I'll make sure you have an extra six buckets to fetch this shift," snapped the guard. "I'll be back after I've checked on the other group, and you'd better not be here when I return."

"Understood," muttered Varl, coughing and clutching his chest.

He waited until the guard disappeared from view and then snapped the cover back in place. He took a quick look at the display—it was still flashing and the numbers looked good. Success! He wondered how long it would be before one of the Gulden Guards noticed the flashing light.

By the time he reached Bronya and Sarven his elation had died. He realized that one flashing indicator would probably not be enough to clear the whole mine—just the lower tunnels. Would Javeer shut down the whole mine if the other meters all read normal levels of methane?

"Thank goodness you're safe," said Bronya, putting her arms around Varl. "I was so worried when we couldn't stall the guard any longer."

"Did you fix the meter?" asked Sarven.

Varl nodded. "I did."

Sarven patted him on the back and looked so happy that Varl hadn't the heart to share his fears. He could only hope that Javeer would stop the mining operations while they checked out the situation.

Varl picked up his air hammer and set to work. Today they had to be done on time. He wanted to get out of the shaft and near the huge fans. Perhaps then he could really raise the levels of methane in the mine.

* * * * *

Matt rubbed his lower back, regretting that he had slept on such a hard and uneven surface. But considering he'd probably had less than three hours' sleep he did feel surprisingly refreshed, which was important on such a big day. He looked at his watch with disbelief. They had slept for eight hours, not three!

"Varak, Keir, wake up! We've got problems."

"What problems?" Varak mumbled, still half asleep.

Keir sat up and rubbed the back of his neck. "What a rough hour's sleep."

"Hour?" said Matt. "We've been asleep for *eight* hours!"

"You're kidding!" said Keir. "How did we manage that?"

"It's called exhaustion," said Matt as he picked up his sweater and shoved it in his pack. "But now we're in trouble. We've missed the smaller night shift. By the time we get to where the old and new tunnels connect we're likely to bump into lots of Gulden Guards on the big first shift."

"Great," groaned Varak. "Our task will be harder with more people and more guards."

"But not impossible," said Keir with surprising optimism.

"Agreed," said Matt. "We'll continue, of course."

"Of course," said Varak, slinging on his pack and setting off.

As they trudged along the hangingwall got lower and lower until they couldn't walk, even with bent backs.

"Crawling time," announced Varak. "That means we must be close."

The gap became so low that Matt could only just crawl with his backpack on. He made slow progress with a flashlight in one hand and his pack sliding around on his back. The attached shovel banged his side every few feet.

"Hope we don't have to do this for too long," he said. "My arms and knees are killing me."

Varak paused for a rest. "I know what you mean. It can't be far now."

Sure enough, within minutes the tunnel came to an end. "Okay, this is it," said Varak.

"Now what?" asked Keir.

"Now we dig," said Varak. "I reckon that Javeer's shafts should be only a few feet away on the other side of this wall of rock."

"What if you're wrong?" said Keir. "I mean, let's face it, you're just guessing, aren't you?"

Varak groaned. "Well, if I'm wrong, I'm wrong. We'll just find one of the other old entrances and try again."

"Digging will be slow work when we can't even stand up," said Keir.

"We could do with the Gnashers again," said Matt.

"They would sure make this job a lot easier," said Varak. "But we don't know where they are and we haven't got any way of getting them here."

"If the Gnashers can communicate with us by sending us pictures, perhaps we can send messages to them using pictures," said Matt.

"It's worth a try," said Varak.

"I'm for anything that saves us having to dig," said Keir. "But I suggest we move back from the rock wall first."

"Good point," said Matt. He waited for Keir to turn and crawl back twenty feet and then followed. "Okay. Let's see what we can do." He got out his laptop from his pack and turned it on. The opening scenes from the Keeper game appeared. Matt was thankful that neither Keir nor Varak had a clear view of the screen in the cramped tunnel, or they'd probably ask some hard questions.

Matt scrolled down the menu looking for options that might be useful in this scenario of his game. He read down the list: *Maps, Transportation, Underground, Runner, Food, Supplies, Weapons, Help* and *Keeper.* Nothing seemed appropriate. He read them all a second time and decided *'Maps'* was his only reasonable choice. His stomach knotted when the screen appeared. Yet again someone else had opened up this section of his game before him. How was this happening? Who was this other player?

"How are you going to contact the Gnashers?" asked Keir.

"Not sure yet," mumbled Matt. "I'm hoping that sending the Gnashers a map of the mine might work. It's kind of like a picture."

"You've got maps of the mine?" said Varak, raising his voice.

Matt instantly realized his mistake. "Er . . . I didn't bother mentioning it before because they're only some very basic plans from Gova—nothing like the detailed ones that you have." He prayed that Varak would accept his answer and not ask more questions.

"Oh," said Varak. He was silent for a moment. "Well, you'll have to mark where we are on the map. Otherwise the Gnashers won't know where to find us."

Matt was relieved at Varak's response. "You're right," he said, even though he knew he had no way to do that. The maps were part of his game and he couldn't alter them. Besides, the Gnashers had found them last time when they'd needed help. Why not this time?

Matt bit his lip as he searched through the maps. There were five sections: *The Colony of Javeer, The Boro-Boro River, The Dark End of Javeer, The East End of Javeer,* and yes, there it was . . . *Horando Javeer's Gold Mine.*

"Here we go," said Matt, opening up the first of three maps in that section. "This one's no good, it shows the location of the mine and the mountains."

"Been there, done that," said Keir with a laugh.

Matt sighed heavily. "The second is no good, either. It's a map of the buildings above us."

"But it might be useful later," said Varak.

Matt took a deep breath as he opened the third map. "Yes!" he shouted. "We're in luck. It's a plan showing where all the old shafts end."

"So how are you going to let the Gnashers know where we are?" asked Keir.

"Watch," Matt said, tilting the screen towards Keir. He moved the cursor so that it pointed to their location. "Okay, I've only got intermittent wireless reception down here so let's hope it holds out long enough for them to pick it up."

Keir focused the beam of his flashlight down the tunnel. Matt kept his hand steady on the cursor and tried to wait patiently. Time seemed to stand still in the darkness. Then, after what seemed an eternity, specks of gold glinted in the distance.

"You've done it! They're coming!" shouted Keir.

Matt felt relief more than excitement. The Gnashers had saved them from the huge, time-consuming job of chipping their way through a wall of rock without any idea of how far they had to go.

"Lie flat and cover your heads," instructed Varak as the Gnashers drew near.

Matt hurriedly closed his laptop and put it in his pack for protection from the dust. He had just got himself settled face down, arms crossed over his head, when he heard the now familiar high-pitched screech. The Gnashers were already at work.

He coughed as the thick dust swirled around them and the piercing sound drilled through his head. If it was taking the Gnashers this long to get through the rock, Matt knew that he and his friends would not have succeeded with shovels alone.

The sound stopped. Matt lifted his head and felt fresh cooler air blow across his face. His heart raced—surely fresh air meant they had reached the new, ventilated tunnels of Javeer's mineshaft. As he got to his feet to investigate, the Gnashers returned through the tunnel and then disappeared into the blackness behind him.

Matt shone his flashlight through the hole they had created, but he couldn't see past the curve. "I think it goes all the way through, but I've no idea how long it is. You both ready to go?" he whispered.

Keir leaned over Matt's shoulder. "The real question is: are we ready for any Gulden Guards waiting on the other side?"

Chapter 17

"Gnashers!" screamed Sarven, so loudly that Varl dropped his air hammer. It crashed to the floor, sending a cloud of dust up his nose.

Varl sneezed and turned around in time to see dozens of golden balls shooting out of a huge hole that had suddenly appeared in the rock wall. He ducked, more as a natural reflex than from fear. The high-pitched screech bore though his skull and made his head pound.

Sarven was curled up in a ball on the floor and shaking violently, his head tucked as far under his body as Varl thought was humanly possible. Bronya seemed to be in a trance. She stood pressed against the wall of the shaft, her eyes wide and her breath coming in heavy gasps. And yet amidst the noise and the panic Varl felt an amazing sense of calm.

He wasn't sure why—perhaps it was because he'd just learned about these creatures a couple of days ago, and he'd never seen the gruesome evidence of their killing. Or perhaps it was something more. It was almost as if they were whispering to him to have no fear.

After several minutes, most of the Gnashers disappeared back down the hole that they had created. A few continued to circle overhead. Varl allowed himself to look up at the creatures. They had wide mouths showing horrific teeth, just as Sarven had described, and although he felt as if they were watching him, he now realized they had no eyes.

Varl looked at his arms and legs. No teeth marks visible. "Sarven, it's okay. They're not attacking us. You can get up."

Sarven didn't move. Varl shook him. "Sarven, it's okay. You can get up," he said again. Finally he grabbed Sarven's wrist and yanked him to his feet.

Sarven's eyes were fixed on the few Gnashers that remained, his face ashen. Varl could feel the boy's blood furiously pumping where he held his wrist.

"You're okay, boy," said Varl. "In fact we're all okay. Look, they're not attacking us. Bronya's okay too, see?"

Bronya also had her eyes on the circling Gnashers, but she began to move slowly towards the tunnel that had just been created. "Isn't this amazing? How do they do it?"

"Silicon-based life forms, I suspect," said Varl. "Simply put, they feed on rock."

"For real?" said Sarven, swallowing hard.

Varl slapped him on the back. "So the good news is that they won't be feeding on you anytime soon."

"Very funny," said Sarven, his voice quaking. "But that doesn't mean that they won't kill me, just that they won't eat me!"

"Where do you think the tunnel leads?" asked Bronya.

Varl peered down the hole. "Without any maps or real knowledge of the Gnashers, I wouldn't like to guess."

Bronya started to climb inside. She turned and looked at Varl. Her eyes were bright with excitement. "This could be our escape route. I don't want to stay in this awful place one minute more than I have to."

"Bronya, don't go, please," begged Sarven. "The Gnashers may not like it. It's their tunnel. They might attack us if we go down it."

"Hold on!" said Varl, grabbing Bronya's ankle. "Let's think about this a minute. The last thing we want to do is end up in a worse situation."

"What could be worse than this?" asked Bronya. "We could all die tomorrow."

"We have no food and hardly any water, and we have no idea where this leads," said Varl. "It's already unbearably hot down here, even though we're in a shaft that's ventilated. That hole *isn't* ventilated. And, as Sarven has pointed out, the Gnashers created this hole or tunnel. At the moment they're leaving us alone. We don't want to upset them by going down it if they don't want us to."

"There's a light flickering down there!" said Bronya, quickly scooting backward and finding the ground.

Varl stuck his head inside to investigate. "It's getting stronger. That means someone or something is coming this way. Get back . . . now!"

They stood in a row facing the hole. Varl picked up his air hammer. It was no match for an ST29, but it did make a deafening noise, and the rotating end could easily cause injury. He held it in front of him as if it were a weapon. Sarven and Bronya copied him.

The light got brighter. Varl could see shadows moving on the walls of the huge tunnel. But he couldn't hear voices, just the sound of scuffling and dragging. Whatever or whoever this was, it was close. He wondered how many more surprises his old heart could take. Having seen the Gnashers appear from nowhere only minutes before, Varl could not imagine what would appear before him next.

The answer came a few seconds later. What seemed to be a human form appeared from the darkness, and finally a face popped out of the hole. Varl dropped his air hammer as a lump rose in his throat and tears welled in his eyes. Was he dreaming?

"Matt, my boy!" he gasped. "Is it really you?"

"It is, it's Matt!" said Bronya, laying her air hammer down. She rushed forward and helped Matt free his backpack and slither hands first from the tunnel onto the dusty floor.

"Varl! Bronya! Thank goodness you're both okay." Matt slipped off his pack and hugged them both. "This is the best news I've had in days."

A second face appeared from the tunnel.

"Keir Logan, I knew you'd rescue me!" Bronya screamed happily.

"Shh!" said Sarven. "Keep your voices low. We don't want Gulden Guards down here."

Keir landed with a thump and a half-somersault in the dust. Bronya curled her arms around her brother's neck and planted several kisses on his cheeks.

"Hang on a minute!" said Keir with a laugh. "Let me

get up before you strangle me." He brushed himself down and cuddled his sister.

"Nice to meet you, Keir," said Varl, stretching out his hand. "Bronya has told me a lot about you. I'm so thankful that you found Matt."

"Could someone help me, please?" said Varak, struggling to get out of the tunnel.

Keir turned around and freed his friend's wedged backpack. "Sorry, we forgot about you in our excitement."

"I'll say you did," said Varak.

Bronya caught hold of Varak's arm and helped to lower him to the floor. "Easy does it—it's quite a drop coming face first."

"How about proper introductions?" said Varak, after he'd straightened himself. Then he stopped and his jaw dropped. "Bro, is that you?" he whispered

Sarven, who had been talking to Matt, turned around and rushed forward. "Varak!"

Tears streamed down Varak's face. "I thought I'd never see you again, bro."

"And I thought I'd be the next in the family to die in this god-forsaken place," said Sarven.

Varak hugged his brother. "Finally some good news for our family."

Varl bent down beside Matt, who was fiddling with his laptop. Varl lowered himself onto the floor next to him. "Problems?"

Matt nodded. "No reception down here. The Gnashers have been helping us but we've communicated using wireless signals. I had a faint signal a while back but now that we're even deeper I've lost it."

"Then we'll just have to get you and your laptop above ground if we need to use the Gnashers again," said Varl.

"That'll be difficult," said Matt. "There must be hundreds of Gulden Guards in these mines."

"No, actually. There are very few down here because they're terrified of the Gnashers. But there are more guards on the next level up, more by the elevator and plenty above ground."

"That's right, I'd forgotten," said Matt. "The Gnashers only attack the guards, not the workers."

"That explains a lot," said Varl. He looked up at the circling Gnashers. "After hearing all those horror stories from Sarven, I wondered why they didn't attack us. It's a pity that he and Bronya didn't know that the Gnashers only attack guards. I can see that you've done well playing Level 4 without me. There's obviously a lot I don't know. You'd better fill me in."

"I can't wait," said Matt. "It's been really hard without you and Targon. I've missed you both terribly. Do you know where Targon is?"

Varl shook his head. "No one seems to have seen him."

* * * * *

Targon cringed as he watched Jake confidently clicking the mouse and moving the cursor. Matt's brother was getting too cocky. Now was not the time to make a mistake. After several hours of playing they were close to finishing the game. This was the final scenario . . . the moment when they freed the people of Boro, crushed Javeer and sent him home. He was not about to lose at the last minute.

"Boy, am I getting good!" said Jake as if to confirm Targon's fears.

"Look, Jake, anyone can make a mistake at any time," said Targon, raising his voice. "Just when you think you've won is when you'll lose. So, have some patience and let's do this carefully."

"Give it a rest, Targon," snapped Jake. "I'm nearly there. Just look at the points I've racked up and all those stupid riddles I've solved. Have faith, man!"

Targon could feel his anger rising. *I've solved?* What had happened to *we*? Hadn't they both been playing the game and solving the clues? *They* had nearly beaten the level. He sighed but held his tongue. The last thing he wanted to do was upset Jake and have him sulk and storm off before they had finished the game.

"Okay, so what's next?" asked Jake.

Targon drew in a deep breath. That was good to hear. Jake was finally asking his advice.

"Well, what have we still got to do to beat the level? Matt and Keir are in the mine and they're working with the Gnashers. That's good because that was an important part of the last rhyme. They've just met up with Varl and Bronya, and Varl's fixed one of the methane gas meters to read high. That's even better. So what's left?"

"The ventilation fans," said Jake. "We've got to destroy them once the workers are clear of the mine."

"Right. And after that the levels of gas should rise quickly and create an explosion that'll end Javeer's whole mining business."

"So, let's get to it," said Jake. "I'll click on '*Weapons*.' We've plenty of points to pick up some explosives to destroy the fans. I'll create one mighty load of fireworks—you'll see!"

"Wait!" said Targon as Jake was about to click on Number 7, '*Weapons*.' "There are several problems with using explosives." Jake was weapon-crazy and that scared him. Things could quickly get out of hand.

"Like what?" said Jake in a gruff voice. "You need something that'll put the fans out of action for a long time, and if you ask me, blowing 'em up is the best way to do that. Kaboom!" Jake made the swooshing sound of an explosion. "We might get lucky and take out a few Gulden Guards as well."

Targon sighed. "And what about all the workers that live in the bunkhouses nearby? What are we going to do—get them all out of the mine safely just to kill them on the surface?"

Jake shrugged. "That's okay. Sometimes one of the good guys has to die to save the rest. It happens in lots of movies and games."

"We're not talking about one person—we're talking about hundreds!" said Targon, hardly believing what he had just heard. "You can't seriously want to risk the lives of hundreds of innocent workers!"

"Chill, man!" said Jake. "See the computer? See the CD box? See the instruction booklet?" He picked up the booklet and waved it in front of Targon's face. "It's only a game."

Targon's blood boiled. If only it *were* just a game. "Anyway, the rhyme was very specific," he suddenly blurted out.

"How do you mean?"

"It said '*destroy the pithead and you won't succeed.*' Don't you remember?"

"So? We're destroying the fans, not the whole pithead," argued Jake.

"But none of the characters have experience in planting explosives. That means that things could easily go wrong. Set off too big an explosion and the whole place goes up. Then we lose because we didn't follow the clues."

"Okay, brains, you win. No explosives," said Jake in an angry tone. "I hope you've got a better idea."

"Yes, actually I have," lied Targon. *What better idea? Think quickly, Targon!*

"Well?" said Jake.

And then it came to him . . . "Gnashers—let's use the Gnashers! Remember the rhyme? It said '*Use the Gnashers if you dare*' and '*with their Keeper fight a common foe.*' We've only used them to eat through the rock, so why don't we use them in the final scenario against Javeer?"

"Yeah, right," said Jake. He groaned. "So how do you propose we do this?"

Targon was racking his brains. He had no idea.

Chapter 18

Matt's stomach was churning with worry in spite of the euphoric atmosphere in the mine. He was really worried about Targon now that he knew that Varl hadn't seen him either. Varak had been reunited with Sarven, and Keir had found Bronya. How he wished that Targon had been here too. With all that they had been through together, Targon was more than a good friend—he was like a brother. It pained Matt that he might have failed him in some way. Was Targon in another part of Boro or had he ended up somewhere else entirely? It was a scary thought because Matt had no idea how to locate him or how to get him back.

And now he'd lost his ability to communicate with the Gnashers. Things had gone so well up to this point—why couldn't his run of good luck have continued?

Still, finding Varl gave him some comfort. Varl, too, was like family, and he'd really missed him. Even better, by tampering with one of the gas meters, Varl had already helped him with the final phase of Level 4. It had been wonderful to sit down and strategize with him again. Together they'd decided on what they must do next and he felt confident that their plan would succeed. He had to put Targon out of his mind for now and concentrate on winning Level 4.

Matt looked up at the Gnashers and counted. There were six that had remained and they were still circling above. Everyone else had forgotten about them with the excitement of the reunions. Even Sarven, who'd been desperately fearful of the Gnashers, seemed oblivious. Matt couldn't help but wonder why those six had stayed. How he wished his laptop would work so that he could find out.

Suddenly a horn blared through the tunnels, giving Matt a jolt. Varl had told him that one long single blast signified the end of the shift, but these were continuous shorter blasts.

"Okay," said Varl. "My guess is that this is an emergency signal to clear the mine. It's time to make our move. We'll split up and say our goodbyes." He paused. "Matt, you look great dressed as Sarven—very convincing."

"Yes, his clothes do fit me well," said Matt. He squeezed his laptop into Sarven's smaller green canvas backpack. The corners stuck out through the fabric. He hoped that the guards wouldn't notice the rectangular shape.

Varak handed him the tools he'd been carrying. "Some of this stuff might come in handy."

Matt nodded and stuffed what he could in front of the laptop. He lifted the backpack. As he'd suspected, it was heavy. "Do I look okay?" he asked.

"As I said, you look just like Sarven," said Varl. "None

of the Gulden Guards will know the difference. You're about the same height and we've only been here two days, so they've not had time to get to know us yet."

Sarven laughed. "We've done a good job dirtying your hair with rock dust. It's so black that you can't tell you're blond. If you keep your helmet on, no one will know that you're not me."

"Don't worry," said Varl. "The guards will be so eager to get out, they'll just count bodies going up in the cage. So, is everyone clear on what we are doing? Sarven, Varak and Keir are to make their way out of the mine through the old tunnels and go to Mrs. Morsova's cottage. Bronya and Matt are coming with me to the pithead where we'll stop Javeer's mining once and for all."

"Sorry I can't stay and watch your back, old man," said Sarven.

"No problem," said Varl. "You've done plenty for me already."

Sarven's lower lip quivered as he shook Varl's hand. "We'll be waiting for you at Aunt Leila's."

"We'll be there," replied Varl.

Keir hugged his sister. "I wish there were another way, Bron. I hate letting you go again when I've just found you."

"I'll be fine," said Bronya. "I'm stronger than you think."

Keir nodded. "I can see that. I'm sorry I didn't involve you in the Underground before. It wasn't that I didn't think you were capable or trustworthy, it's just that I was thinking of Ma and Nadia. They need you. I wish I could go with Varl instead of you."

"You can't go instead of me," said Bronya. "I got a reputation as a trouble-maker when I put up a fight against Javeer. They'll notice immediately if I'm missing. If I leave the mine right now the Gulden Guards might come looking for me and find the Gnashers' tunnel. It'll draw suspicion on Varl and Matt, and the plan won't work."

Despite her confident words, Matt could tell that Bronya was putting on a brave face. It would have been so easy for her to give in and go home with Keir.

"Thank you, Bronya, for putting the fate of the citizens of Boro above your own," said Varak in a very dignified manner. He shook her hand firmly. "Thousands are depending on you."

"Matt and Bronya, let's get going," said Varl. "Sarven, Varak and Keir, you must be on your way too. We'll see you soon."

Bronya turned and gave her brother a weak smile as she followed Varl up the shaft toward the supplies area.

After only a few minutes Matt was dripping with sweat despite carrying only a backpack and the air hammer. He wondered how Varl, Bronya and Sarven had managed to carry so many heavy buckets of rock back and forth in the heat. His journey into the mine had been all downhill or on the level. Going uphill was far harder even with the ventilation system blasting fresh air from outside.

Matt couldn't believe the commotion as he approached the desk to hand over his supplies. The workers must have been told why the sirens were blaring because they were almost throwing their equipment at the guards and running up the shafts toward the elevators, pushing and shoving each other out of the way. The three guards on duty behind the desk didn't seem to care.

Matt put his air hammer down and then realized that he had to hand over his helmet as well. Fear knotted inside him. Would any of the Gulden Guards realize when he took off the helmet that he shouldn't be with the group? He waited until the guard in front of him was occupied taking another worker's equipment, then removed his helmet and lay it on the bench. He was about to make a hasty retreat when he spotted an ST29 propped against the side of the desk.

His heart quickened. Dare he take it? How useful an ST29 would be. Could he take it without being caught? He looked up and met Varl's gaze. Varl had seen it too. Did he think it a good idea or not?

"Hey, you!" one of the guards shouted. "I've never seen you before. What bunkhouse are you in?"

Matt froze. He had been spotted. In that moment he decided. He grabbed the ST29, backed himself against the wall of the shaft and pointed it unsteadily at the two guards standing next to the hoppers twenty feet away. Both had their ST29s drawn and pointed at him.

The workers screamed and the crowd parted, leaving Matt to face the guards, a clear expanse between them. It was like a scene out of a western movie. Time seemed to slow. In spite of the blaring sirens all Matt heard was silence.

He could see Varl and Bronya staring at him, horror

written across their faces. He could not expect them to help—the last thing Matt wanted to do was to ruin their whole plan. This was something he had to do on his own, and he could see in Varl's eyes that he was thinking the same.

"It's useless, boy," said one of the guards behind the desk, his lips twisted into a cynical smile. "It's five against one and four of us are armed." He fiddled with one of his golden earrings as if he had all the time in the world.

Matt's mind was in turmoil. How was he going to get out of this one?

Just as he had given up hope of getting out of this alive, he saw a flash of gold out of the corner of his left eye . . . and then another and another. It was a beautiful sight: six golden Gnashers speeding to his aid. Now Matt understood why some of the Gnashers had stayed. They had stayed to protect him.

"Gnashers!" bellowed Matt.

The guards' expressions changed immediately, terror showing on their unshaven faces. They fired at the attacking creatures but with no effect. Matt watched as the Gnashers circled closer and closer to the guards, their terrifying teeth bared. One by one the Gulden Guards dropped their weapons and screamed as they ran down the shafts, hotly pursued by the flying golden spheres.

Matt shuddered. He was glad he was not going to witness the rest.

"Matt, give me the weapon and let's go, right now!" said Varl, hardly giving him time to take in what had happened. "We've been given a small window of opportunity to do what we've got to do, so let's make the most of it."

Matt was pleased to hand him the ST29. Varl seemed to have found new life in his old bones as they ran up the narrow tunnels. Brandishing the ST29 he cleared a path for Matt and Bronya through the masses waiting at the base of the elevator shaft.

The buzzer sounded. No one questioned them when the elevator arrived and Varl pushed the three of them to the front of the line, followed by twelve others. More workers tried to force their way into the cage in desperation but Varl pointed the weapon at them and shouted, "Fifteen's the limit." Matt hated to behave like that but he figured that on this occasion their mission justified it.

"Get into the middle of the group and stay with them past the ventilation fans and the first two bunkhouses," whispered Varl as the elevator rose. "Then follow me."

The moment they reached the surface and the doors to the cage were opened, Matt positioned himself between several workers and behind Varl and Bronya. The brutal cold cut through him after the heat he had just endured. Keeping his head down he shuffled past the two Gulden Guards on duty. But no more than twenty steps later, everyone came to a halt. He looked up to see a tiny man in tight green leggings striding toward them.

Bronya turned her head and hastily warned him, "It's Horando Javeer, and I can tell he's looking for me."

Matt immediately inched sideways and hid himself behind a tall man. He peered around the worker's arm and stared at the strange figure who stood in front of her. So this was Horando Javeer. Who would have guessed? How could such a small ugly man command so much fear and hold a nation to ransom?

He felt anxious, more for Bronya than for himself. Varl had told him how Bronya had bravely stood up to the squeaky dictator only to be beaten in front of everyone. He admired the girl and wondered if she would be able to keep calm knowing that their plan was at stake.

"Bronya Logan," screeched Javeer. "I trust you are enjoying working for me."

Bronya lowered her head. "Yes, Keeper," she replied.

Horando Javeer seemed taken aback by her response. He hesitated, frowned and then said, "Good. I'm glad to see that two days of working in my mines has put out the fire in you, young lady. Now perhaps you will see reason and give me the answers to my questions."

"And what questions were those, Keeper?" asked Bronya in a subdued voice, her head still down.

"Tell me of the stranger from Gova and the computer that he carries."

Matt felt his chest tighten. Horando Javeer knew about him and his computer! He held his breath waiting for her answer.

"I told you before, Keeper, I know nothing about these things."

Matt flinched. Even he had heard the annoyance in

her voice. He waited anxiously to see what Javeer would say or do next.

Javeer took two steps closer so that he was almost standing on Bronya's toes. His green eyes narrowed and he pointed his index finger at her. Then, slowly and deliberately he pressed his outstretched finger under Bronya's chin and forcefully lifted her head. "Look at me, girl, when I speak to you," he hissed. "You obviously haven't heard that your mother is dying."

Bronya gasped.

Matt could tell that Javeer had gotten the desired response from her. A smile tipped the corners of Javeer's mouth.

"You'd like to be at her side when she passes into the next life, wouldn't you?" he said in a fake compassionate tone.

Matt gulped. Would Bronya take the bait? He wanted to protect her but couldn't. Whatever the outcome of this confrontation, he could not defend her. He had to stay hidden in order to finish his game.

Bronya said nothing. Matt wondered if she'd guessed that Javeer was playing with her emotions.

"I will return you to the Dark End to be with your mother if, and only if, you give me the information I want," said Javeer, impatience in his voice.

Bronya drew in a deep breath. "There is no guarantee, Keeper, that your words are true and that my mother is about to die. I want proof!"

"Proof? You want proof?" bellowed Javeer, his eyes

blazing with anger. "How dare you bargain with me!"

"I'm not intending to bargain with you, Keeper," said Bronya, her voice quavering. "But what reason do I have to trust you?"

Javeer scratched his head vigorously, causing his straggly hair to stick out above his ears. His eyes searched her face and what was only a few seconds of silence seemed like hours to Matt.

"Bronya Logan," he said finally, "the Keeper bargains with no one. You will die in my mine and your mother will die alone."

With that, Javeer turned and marched away as quickly as he had arrived. Bronya hung her head and sobbed.

Matt put his arm around her. She looked pretty, even with tears in her eyes and dirt on her face. "I'm sure that your mother's no worse, Bronya," he consoled. "We'll get Javeer, you'll see—and very soon. He'll regret everything he's ever said and done to you. I'll make sure of that."

Bronya gave him a weak smile. "Thanks."

Matt was filled with so much rage and determination that nothing would prevent him from finishing what he had set out to do.

Chapter 19

Matt hid between two tall workers as the line passed several dozen armed Gulden Guards patrolling up and down in front of the enormous hoppers. The noise was deafening as they approached the roaring ventilation fans. He tried not to appear interested, but it was his first glimpse of Horando Javeer's mining operation and he couldn't help but take a look. The huge electric cables that supplied power to the fans swung in the wind overhead. These were his target.

The mine guide at the front of the line was focused on his job of escorting the prisoners to their bunkhouses. Just ahead of Matt, Varl and Bronya dropped to the back of the group, feigning tiredness. When nobody seemed to notice or care, Matt dropped back too.

"Ready?" whispered Varl.

Matt nodded. "Ready."

"It's the next bunkhouse, number 151. The path goes right down the side of it."

As they turned the corner, out of sight of the Gulden Guards, Varl bent down and with a struggle, squeezed himself under the bunkhouse. Bronya followed him so quickly that Matt hardly noticed her go.

Now it was his turn. His nerves tensed. He shot a quick look at the workers. They continued to follow the mine guide, huddled together in the icy wind, oblivious to what was going on behind them.

Matt removed his backpack, pushed it under the bunkhouse and then slithered on his stomach into the gap between the ground and the bunkhouse floor. It was a tight fit, with little room to move or turn, and hardly any space to lift his head. Varl lay perfectly still next to him and Bronya next to Varl.

Matt lay silently on his stomach in the cold for several minutes, heart racing, afraid to move, expecting to hear the guards shout that prisoners were missing. But they didn't. So far, so good.

"Now?" asked Matt.

"It's time," said Varl.

In the confined space, Matt struggled to reach his backpack and unzip it. He took out his laptop, turned it on and opened up his game. This had to work. "Okay, everyone. Say your prayers. Here's hoping we get a wireless signal."

"Well?" said Bronya.

"Give it a minute," said Matt. He found himself holding his breath as the computer searched. "We have reception," he finally said with relief. He heard long sighs from both Varl and Bronya.

"Now I just need to bring up pictures of the ventilation fans," said Matt, searching through his game instructions. Where would he find such a thing?

"And then we'll hope the Gnashers will pick them up and get to work," added Varl.

"What makes you think that the Gnashers will know what we want them to do?" whispered Bronya.

Matt scooted forward to look at her on the other side of Varl. "It's all chance. But they've come to my rescue three times now. They're definitely out to get rid of Javeer and the Gulden Guards, or why else would they attack them and not us?"

"Matt, get on with it," snapped Varl. "No time to chat."

"Yeah, right," said Matt, turning back to focus on the menu. But again, none of the choices seemed appropriate. He certainly wouldn't find pictures of ventilation fans under *Weapons, Supplies, Food or Transportation*. It had to be Number 1, *'Maps'* again. Hurriedly he searched the files until he found maps of Javeer's gold mine and clicked on the area around the pithead. Sure enough, large photographs of ventilation fans appeared.

"We're in business," said Matt, turning the screen so that Varl could see.

"Perfect," he answered.

Matt zoomed in on the huge electric cables that supplied the fans. That was their target. Would the Gnashers get the message? Now all they could do was wait.

Varl shifted around uncomfortably on the ground and Matt guessed that his arthritis was giving him trouble. This was not the place for an elderly man. Bronya laid her head between her folded arms and closed her eyes, obviously exhausted.

"What? Bronya Logan is missing?" a deep voice bellowed from the corner of the bunkhouse.

Matt froze.

"Darn! That's Captain Culmore," whispered Varl.

"And he'll tear the place apart until he finds us," added Bronya.

"Find her!" continued Culmore. "The Keeper has a special interest in this prisoner. She's to be kept alive at all costs. Do you hear me?"

"Yes, Captain, sir," answered one of the Gulden Guards.

"And get the mine guide who escorted this group from the elevator. Bring him to me immediately!"

"He's here, Captain."

"Are you the mine guide?"

From where he was hidden, Matt could see the feet of the feeble old man. He shuffled nervously from side to side.

"Yes, sir," muttered the guide.

"So what happened to this girl who was in your care?" asked Culmore, his voice strained.

"I don't know, Captain."

"It's your job to know! Your duty is to escort prisoners from the cage back to their bunkhouse. You will join their shift in the mine tomorrow for your negligence!"

"No, please, Captain. I've worked hard for four years and I've nearly done my time here," begged the mine guide. "Don't send me back down there."

"Two others missing from 157, Captain," said the

guard.

"Two others? What two others?" screamed Culmore.

"An elderly man named Varl and a boy, Sarven Morsova," the guard said timidly.

"Get this mine guide out of my sight!" said Culmore. "So there are three missing from the same bunkhouse. What's the betting they're all together? They can't have gone far. I want every guard, on or off duty, to search for them immediately!"

Matt looked at Varl. "What do we do?" he whispered.

"All that we can do. We stay here and hope the Gnashers appear before the guards find us."

Just as Varl finished speaking, Culmore peered under the bunkhouse and pointed his ST29 at them. "Get out from under there, now!" he bellowed, standing upright again.

Matt's heart sank. He felt as though his stomach had risen into his mouth. He watched Varl push the ST29 they had stolen further under the bunkhouse out of sight. A wise move, he thought. They may need it later. He looked at his computer.

"You'll have to take your computer," said Varl, reading his thoughts. "Javeer knows you have it. Once he realizes you aren't Sarven, he'll only send guards to look under here later."

"Get out, I said!" bellowed Culmore a second time.

Matt slithered out and scrambled to his feet, pulling his backpack and the computer out after him. Bronya was already standing, glaring at Culmore with huge burning eyes. He squeezed her hand to offer reassurance but she didn't seem to notice. Her attention was completely focused on Culmore. Varl struggled to his feet, rubbing his back.

Culmore was seething. He stood in front of Matt, tall and angry. His nostrils flared and his eyes darkened like thunderclouds. "What a stupid place to hide," he chuckled nastily. "Didn't you think that this would be the first place we would look?"

Matt flashed him a look of disdain. "It would have been more stupid not to have taken the opportunity to get away from brutes like you."

Culmore's lips thinned with irritation but then curled into a smile as his gaze fell on Matt's computer. "Well, look here! This is my lucky day! You must be the stranger from Gova," he said. "I'll take the computer. The Keeper will be pleased to get this."

Matt's arms tightened around his prize possession, and he hugged it to his chest.

Culmore stepped forward and made a move to grab it from him.

Bronya gasped and pointed to the sky. "It's the Gnashers," she screamed. "Just look at them. There must be hundreds . . . no, thousands coming over the mountain."

Matt could hardly contain his excitement as he saw a flock of golden spheres heading toward them.

Culmore hesitated, obviously not knowing whether to take his attention away from his captives even for a second. But the sky seemed to darken and he looked up. Matt relished the moment. The cruel guard's face reflected panic, confusion and fear.

Culmore made another move to grab Matt's computer but a lone Gnasher flew at his face. He raised his hand to his cheek and stared at the blood on his fingertips. His eyes darted back and forth nervously as the Gnashers drew in closer, circling and swooping like a flock of birds getting ready to roost. A moment later he turned and ran towards the Gulden Guards' accommodation, screaming, "Get out of here! Retreat!"

"I guess he thinks we'll be eaten alive standing out here," said Matt with a laugh. "He probably thinks he'll come back later and find my computer lying on the ground next to my dead body!"

"Don't even joke about things like that," said Bronya.

Matt watched in amazement as the Gnashers began to eat their way through the huge electrical cables, which supplied the ventilation fans. They kept up the attack until each one broke and came swinging down. Silicon-based life forms couldn't be electrocuted because of their rock base, but Matt was aware how close he was standing to the swaying ends of the cables.

"Let's all move back a bit," he said to Varl, just as sparks flew from dangling ends that were making contact with each other. Finally the enormous fans slowed and came to a grinding halt.

"They've done it!" said Bronya. "They've actually done it!"

"How long before enough gas builds up to create an explosion?" asked Matt.

"It could be ten minutes, could be an hour," said Varl.

Matt groaned. "Well, let's hope it's only ten minutes, or Culmore and any surviving guards will be back out here. Any ideas where we should go?"

"How about through the fence?" said Varl.

Matt laughed. "I wish."

He saw Varl's faraway look and turned to see hundreds of Gnashers attacking the three rows of electric fences. They were eating through the wire as easily as humans would bite through a sandwich.

"Unbelievable!" said Matt. "Look at the gap in the fence."

"Let's evacuate the workers," said Varl. "We'll stand a better chance of escaping in a crowd."

"But please, let's stay together," begged Bronya. "I really would like us *all* to get out of here alive."

"Agreed," said Matt, even though he knew it made more sense that they split up. Bronya had been through enough of an ordeal already.

"Okay," said Varl. "Let's do this. We can get the workers out of the first two bunkhouses and then send off some of them to tell the others."

"This one first," said Bronya, flinging open the door.

"Out, everyone," shouted Matt. "We're all free. There's a gap in the fence."

None of the workers moved. They stared at Matt, Varl and Bronya for a second and then continued with their card games and chatter. Still clutching his computer, Matt ran up and down the room, pausing at each table. "Go! All of you, go! Now is your chance." But still he was ignored. He returned to the doorway where Bronya seemed equally confused by the prisoners' behavior.

"What's the problem?" Matt asked Varl.

"Fear. It's fear, pure and simple, my boy," he replied. "Fear of being caught by Javeer and fear of the Gnashers."

Then there was an almighty blast, followed by another stronger blast, and then by a third, even larger than the other two. A low rumbling began, and it got louder and louder until the room shook and the floor beneath them trembled.

"What's happening?" asked Bronya, her eyes wide with fright.

Matt dashed to a window in time to see rocks crashing down the mountain behind the mine. His heart sang with delight. "The mine! We've destroyed it!"

The workers who had refused to move minutes earlier now ran into the street, screaming and yelling.

Matt followed them outside then stopped to take in the scene. To his relief the landslide had crushed the fans and the locomotives outside, but the pithead remained intact just as the rhyme had instructed. As he watched, workers ran from the pithead cage. Now he understood. There were still several hundred workers below the surface, since the cage carried only fifteen at a time. If they had destroyed the pithead all of those people would have died.

Near the mine, hundreds of Gulden Guards looked like rows of tin soldiers standing to attention while assessing the damage. Not one of them seemed bothered by the mass hysteria in the streets behind. And amidst them stood Javeer, staring at the mountainside, a dazed look on his face as if he couldn't quite work out what had happened. Now the tiny man looked truly insignificant amidst the destruction. After all, he was only human.

Varl led them quickly round to the side of bunkhouse 151. He crawled underneath and retrieved the stolen ST29. "It might come in handy," he said as they crossed the street to the elaborate network of security fences.

Matt's stomach was in knots as they passed through the gap created by the Gnashers in the first fence, and raced across the icy ground to the second fence. A wave of apprehension swept over him as they squeezed through the smaller opening in the second. He glanced up at the guard tower by the gate. No Gulden Guards on duty. Now he was within feet of the third fence. Would they actually make it out of here?

Ahead of him, Bronya pushed her way through the last gaping hole, catching her tunic on a piece of protruding wire. Varl quickly freed her and stepped through.

Matt turned to take one last look at the place where Javeer's greed had created so much terror, and then he looked toward the sky. The Gnashers were leaving just as they had arrived. Like a huge, glistening flock of birds, they swooped and swirled until the last had disappeared over the top of the mountain.

"Come on," said Varl, beckoning to him from the other side of the fence. "What's wrong with you? Hurry it up!"

Matt drew in a deep breath and marched through the wire to freedom.

Chapter 20

M att struggled out of the tunnel and across Mrs. Morsova's basement with Varl hanging on his neck. The journey had taken its toll on his elderly friend, whose knees were swollen and painful. Bronya, on the other hand, seemed to have boundless energy even after her ordeal. She could hardly contain her excitement, chattering all the way back about how the Underground Council would have to eat their words, and how her brother would be a hero to everyone in the Dark End. Matt knew he was going to miss her but he hoped that he'd be long gone when she confronted Gorbun. He doubted anyone would forgive those who had turned traitor and worked with the Gulden Guards.

Bronya rushed ahead, climbed the ladder and banged on the trap door. Matt could hear Keir's shouts of joy as he greeted his sister in the kitchen.

Varak hurried down the ladder to help him. "We heard the news," he said excitedly before he had reached the bottom. "It's all over the East End that Javeer's mining is finished and that he's taking the Gulden Guards and leaving Boro. What an exciting day this is! You did a great job."

"I wish you could have been there to see it," said Matt.

"It was total destruction!"

Varak's eyes shone with joy. "Life will be so different from now on. I can't even imagine what it will be like walking down the streets of the East End without fear of being arrested."

"Thanks for your help, my boy," said Varl, freeing himself from Matt, "but I don't think I can make it up the ladder right now. I'll have to stay down here for a while."

"Why don't you go lie down on the bed in that room, through there?" said Varak, pointing to a door. "Make yourself comfortable, and I'll ask Aunt Leila to bring you some of her prize-winning rabbit stew. You'll feel much better in no time."

"Sounds perfect," said Varl, hobbling across the room.

"I'll give you a hand," said Matt, taking Varl's arm and guiding him.

Matt opened the door. He gasped. This was unbelievable! The room looked exactly like his study at home, with paneled walls and built-in bookcases. There were family photographs on the walls and familiar titles on the bookshelves. But something—and he wasn't sure what—didn't seem right.

He sniffed the air. Something smelled familiar—in fact, he could swear he smelled his mother's brownies. His gaze fell on the far corner. Two blond boys were sitting at a desk in front of a computer. When they turned toward him, Matt could not believe his eyes. One looked remarkably like Targon and the other closely resembled Jake! He shut his eyes and shook his head, wondering if exhaustion was causing him to hallucinate. But when he opened his eyes again, he was still standing in a room that *looked like* his study back home, and people who *looked like* Jake and Targon were still sitting at the computer. How was this possible? Was he dreaming or were Targon and his brother really here? Varl answered that thought immediately.

"Targon?" Varl said. "How did you get here?"

At that, Targon got up from his chair and ran toward them. "Varl! Matt! I've been so worried about you both." He hugged each of them. "I can't believe it. I beat Level 4 and now you're safely home."

"Home?" said Matt, eyeing Targon suspiciously. "This isn't home."

Targon frowned. "Of course it is. Your mom's in the kitchen. Can't you hear her singing?"

Matt smiled. He heard someone singing the theme from *Titanic*—there could be no mistaking his mother's sweet soprano voice. "It sounds like her," he said, feeling very confused. How could this be home when he had just walked through Mrs. Morsova's basement? And he certainly hadn't entered the final commands of Level 4 of *Keeper of the Kingdom*. Or had he?

"And your brother, Jake, has been helping me win Level 4," said Targon. I had to do something when you didn't show, so Jake offered to play instead."

Matt walked over to where Jake was sitting. Jake turned and grinned at him. Matt gulped. The boy looked like Jake with his large bulbous nose and long face. He smiled like Jake, silver braces showing out of a cocky twisted mouth, and even his hair was spiked at the crown of his head in the same way. But it couldn't be Jake, could it?

"Whaz up, bro? You sure took ya time getting here," said Jake. "Beat this dumb game of yours, no problem."

"You did?"

"Well, me and Targon did, though I was the one with the skill, of course," said Jake.

Targon glowered. "Don't listen to him," he shouted across the room. "He's weapons mad! If it wasn't for me he'd have ruined the whole of Level 4!"

"Right," said Matt. That sure sounded like Jake, who always went into a game feet first and brains later, but there was something missing—something empty in his eyes.

"Jake?" Matt said. He reached forward to touch Jake's arm and drew it back in horror. His hand seemed to go right through the boy's arm! How was that possible? "You're not Jake! Who are you?"

"I am the second Keeper in Level 4, the Keeper of the Gnashers," said a husky commanding voice that was definitely not Jake's and yet came out of his mouth.

Targon pelted back across the room. "You're what?" he yelled. "You're Jake, Matt's brother. You've been helping me," he said, choking on his words. "Quit joking with me and quit putting on that stupid accent. You're not the Keeper of the Gnashers—you can't be."

"Oh, but I can be . . . and I am. I'm sure you have all

heard of holograms."

"You're a hologram?" Matt asked, his voice shakier than he would have liked. He wasn't sure if he should be frightened of this . . . this thing.

"Yes, I'm a hologram. In fact, this entire room is a hologram recreated for you right down to the smells and, of course, your mother's sweet voice."

"I don't understand," said Matt.

"Humans are too ready to believe what they want to believe."

"But you talked to me," said Targon. "We worked together. You seemed so real."

"Because you wanted me to be real you didn't question it. I'm just an extension of Matt's computer."

"Yeah, really," said Matt skeptically.

"You, Targon, are a character in the game and also a player. For the first three levels of *Keeper of the Kingdom*, you eagerly helped Matt while wishing you could play the game on your own. I was sent here by Matt's computer to fulfill your wish and to make Level 4 more . . . interesting. You were told in the rhyme to work with the Keeper of the Gnashers and that's exactly what you were doing. You were working with me, an extension of Matt's computer, with the ability to control the Gnashers . . . although of course I deliberately made your task harder at times."

Matt felt angry and yet confused. "And we're supposed to believe all of this?"

"You work it out—you're the computer whiz. You should know that computers today are extremely complicated and capable machines, and that computer games are intricate with very detailed realistic graphics."

"But humans build the computers and write the games," said Matt, determined to argue against what seemed so unbelievable.

"Indeed they do. But computers are programmed to think and adapt to different situations. They come up with problems and scenarios that can challenge even the best of programmers. You can't tell me that you haven't ever played against your computer in a game?"

"Lots of times," said Matt. "And I often lose."

"Well then," continued the hologram. "Is this so hard to believe? You have just played against your computer! Now ask yourself, what is the purpose of a computer game?"

Matt shrugged. "To give me a challenge while I have fun."

The hologram laughed. "That and to keep you playing—to keep you coming back time and time again. You humans get so involved in the games that you play that eventually the real world fades into the background. You don't even hear anything in the real world around you. All you see is what is on the screen and all you hear are the noises of the game. Eventually you feel that you are there."

Matt gulped. That part was true.

"*Keeper of the Kingdom* was getting too easy for you, Matthew Hammond. That's why your computer created a two-player two-keeper scenario with lots of twists to keep you interested. You and Targon did well to succeed."

"So we have won, then," said Matt. "We've beaten Level 4 and I can go home. In fact, now that I think about it, I wanted to go home last time and I pressed *'Exit.'* So why didn't the game end?"

The hologram laughed so hard that he appeared to shake. "Think about what I have just said about the human mind, Matthew Hammond. Did you really press *'Exit'* last time, or did your hand do something else at the last minute? The question is, do you *really* want to finish the game right now or would you *really* like to go on and play Level 5?"

Epilogue

Matt looked at Varl for an answer to the hologram's question. Did he want to continue with *Keeper of the Kingdom*? He couldn't believe he was actually thinking about this! Go on and play Level 5? Was he mad? Wasn't it time to go home?

Varl threw his hands up in the air. "It's not up to me," he said with a grin. "But I'll be fit to carry on when I've had a rest."

Targon's face was alight with a beaming smile that stretched from ear to ear. "I know what I'd do," he said decisively. "We're a team. Look what we've done together. I just love these adventures."

Matt turned back to talk to the hologram, but the room was suddenly empty except for a single bed covered with a dark gray blanket, and an old desk and rusty swivel chair in the corner. He ran back to the door and peeked outside. Sure enough, there was the old table in the middle of Mrs. Morsova's basement, the tunnel that led to the East End and the rickety steps up to the kitchen.

Matt shut the door slowly. Then without a word he knelt down on the floor and pulled his laptop out of his backpack. It was time to enter the final commands and finish Level 4 properly.

As pictures of Gulden Guards and Gnashers flashed before him, Matt had still not made his decision. His hand shook when the question, 'Do you wish to continue on *expert difficulty?'* appeared on the screen. He could feel his adrenaline kicking in. His heart was racing and the palms of his hands were sweaty as his fingers hovered above the keys. This game was addictive, for sure.

He looked up at his friends. Varl smiled in a calm, reassuring way and Targon looked at him with beseeching eyes. Was he ready to say goodbye to them both or should he play just one more level? It was an easy decision—especially when he knew that he'd be playing against his computer as well. How could he resist another challenge?

About the Author

H.J. Ralles lives in a Dallas suburb with her husband, two teenage sons and a devoted black Labrador. Keeper of the Colony is her sixth novel.

Visit H.J. Ralles at her website www.hjralles.com

Also by H.J. Ralles

The Keeper Series

Keeper of the Kingdom

Book I

ISBN 1-929976-03-8 Top Publications

In 2540AD, the Kingdom of Zaul is an inhospitable world controlled by Cybergon 'Protectors' and ruled by 'The Keeper'. Humans are 'Worker' slaves, eliminated without thought. Thank goodness this is just a computer game – or is it? For Matt, the Kingdom of Zaul becomes all too real when his computer jams and he is sucked into the game. Now he is trapped, hunted by the Protectors and hiding among the Workers to survive. Matt must use his knowledge of computers and technology to free the people of Zaul and return to his own world. *Keeper of the Kingdom* is a gripping tale of technology out of control.

Keeper of the Realm

Book II
ISBN 1-929976-21-6 Top Publications, Ltd.

In 2540 AD, the peaceful realm of Karn, 300 feet below sea level, has been invaded by the evil Noxerans. This beautiful city has become a prison for the Karns who must obey Noxeran regulations or die at their hands. In the second thrilling adventure of the Keeper Series, Matt uncovers the secrets of the underwater world. He must rid the realm of the Noxerans and destroy the Keeper. But winning level two of his game, without obliterating Karn, looks to be an impossible task. Can Matt find the Keeper before it's too late for them all?

Keeper of the Empire

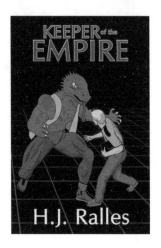

Book III
ISBN 1-929976-25-9 Top Publications, Ltd.

The Vorgs have landed! They're grotesque, they spit venom and Matt is about to be their next victim. What are these lizard-like creatures doing in Gova? Why are humans wandering around like zombies? In the third book of the Keeper series, Matt finds himself in a terrifying world. With the help of his friend Targon, and a daring girl named Angel, Matt must locate the secret hideout of the Govan Resistance. And what has become of the wise old scientist, Varl? There is no end to the action and excitement as Matt attempts to track down the Keeper, and win the next level of his computer game.

The Darok Series

Darok 9

Book I
ISBN 1-929976-10-0 Top Publications, Ltd.

In 2120 AD, the barren surface of the moon is the only home that three generations of earth's survivors have ever known. Towns, called Daroks, protect inhabitants from the extreme lunar temperatures. But life is harsh. Hank Havard, a young scientist, is secretly perfecting SH33, a drug that eliminates the body's need for water. When his First Quadrant laboratory is attacked, Hank saves his research onto a memory card and runs from the enemy. Aided by Will, his teenaged nephew, and Maddie, Will's computer-wizard classmate, Hank must conceal SH33 from the dreaded Fourth Quadrant. But suddenly Will's life is in danger. Who can Hank trust-and is the enemy really closer to home?

Darok 10

Book II
ISBN 1-929976-31-3 Top Publications, Ltd.

Dr. Gunter Schumann has mysteriously vanished from the lunar colony, Darok 9. Was he kidnapped? And what is the significance of the sinister discovery by scientist Hank Havard and Will, his fourteen-year-old nephew? Determined to solve the mystery, Will and his friend Maddie travel to neighboring Darok 10 in search of the truth. But when Will is captured by a ruthless killer bent on destroying the Daroks, Maddie and Hank are forced to steal military secrets. Can they prevent a lunar war and the destruction of humankind?